MOUNTAIN
RAILS
OF OLD

Elaine L. Orr

MOUNTAIN RAILS OF OLD

ELAINE L. ORR

BOOK 3 OF THE
FAMILY HISTORY MYSTERY SERIES

Mountain Rails of Old is a work of fiction. All characters
and story lines are products of the author's imagination.

Lifelong Dreams Publishing

www.elaineorr.com
www.elaineorr.blogspot.com
ISBN 13: 978-1-948070-78-2
Library of Congress Control Number: 2021912825

DEDICTION

For George Fisher, another part of my extended family gone too soon.

To every family historian who has had to explain why they troop in graveyards and cheer when they find records of someone born several centuries ago.

ACKNOWLEDGMENTS

Since I again could not travel to Maryland to do research, I'm grateful for books of others. There is an excellent history of the Civil War in the region in Garrett County: A History of Maryland's Tableland by Stephen Schlosnagle and the Garrett County Bicentennial Committee. His Promised Land is the autobiography of John P. Parker, a former slave and conductor on the Underground Railroad (edited by Stuart Seely Sprague). I also used The Liberty Line: The Legend of the Underground Railroad, by Larry Gara. While the Railroad is not a predominant part of this book, I wanted a better understanding of it, and these were excellent resources.
Thanks to members of the Decatur Critique Group and beta readers – Angela, Dave, Karen, Sue A. and Sue H.

.

CHAPTER ONE

EARLY SPRING IN THE mountains of Western Maryland meant sunshine, the smell of soil, and buds that promised dazzling flowers. Most of all, it signaled air someone could breathe without chilling their lungs, and Digger Browning relished it.

Pleasant temperatures also meant outdoor activities, so on Saturday, Digger and Marty Hofstedder hiked up Meadow Mountain. They had almost reached their destination, a huge boulder that sat atop a ridge. She nudged his elbow with her own. "Fifty cents says you can't climb on top of The Knob."

He grunted. "Ten cents says I'm smart enough not to try to scale the darn thing."

They continued in companionable silence as Bitsy, Digger's German Shepherd, raced past them on the narrow path.

Digger shrugged out of her coat and slung it over her shoulders. "Too early for rabbits."

"I've never known your dog to need an excuse to run around."

"True."

They reached the seven-foot boulder and leaned their backs into it. Marty grabbed Digger's hand. "You're more out of breath than I am."

She laughed. "Says who?"

"Anyone within ten feet of us." He squeezed her hand and let go. "I'm glad you showed me this place."

"Sometimes I forget you didn't grow up here. For a while this was kind of a lover's lane, albeit on foot, but the parks department removed the stones that were comfortable enough to sit on."

Marty raised his eyebrows. "Lover's lane, huh. Now I know why you brought me here."

Digger was enough shorter that she had to stand on her toes to reach him for a quick kiss. She didn't say "dream on," because she wanted to spend time, maybe a few hours or weeks, getting to know him better. But when could they be together privately?

When Digger inherited the Ancestral Sanctuary from Uncle Benjamin, it didn't initially come with his ghost as a permanent resident. As he explained it, when the last shovel of dirt fell on his coffin in the family plot, he found himself sitting atop his and Aunt Clara's large headstone.

She loved the ornery – and no longer aging – octogenarian, but the thought of making love to Marty in the house where he roamed through the walls did not appeal to her. He respected her privacy, but he was simply…there.

How could she explain Uncle Benjamin? A few months ago, she'd taken Marty to the small cemetery behind the house and they'd stood before Aunt Clara's and Uncle Benjamin's headstone. She'd asked Marty what he thought would happen if the sole person who could see a ghost told others about the apparition's existence.

He had to know who she meant. But he also thought she was overwhelmed because of Uncle Benjamin's death and the sudden responsibility for a four-acre property and nearly 100-year-old house. They didn't discuss it more.

Bitsy bounded toward them, tongue hanging out and a bunch of leaves and small sticks on his coat. Marty bent over to brush him off. "What have you been rolling in?"

"Careful. Sometimes dogs roll in gifts left by other dogs."

Marty snatched his hand back and studied it. "Not this time." He grinned and pushed his glasses further up his nose. "It's cold just standing here and it's what, half a mile to the car?"

"Closer to three-quarters, I think." She swung her coat back over her shoulders. "It is getting chilly."

As they walked, Marty spotted a small structure behind a grouping of trees. "I didn't notice that on the way up here."

Digger stopped. "It's a cottage, long since boarded up. If you could see about a quarter-mile farther, you'd see a large frame house with a huge brick chimney. I think the daughter of the people who own that used to live in the cottage."

Marty stepped a couple feet off the path. "Wish I'd brought my camera."

"I don't think the place is going anywhere."

Bitsy growled.

Digger turned. "What is it, Boy?"

Bitsy stared, rigid, ahead of him. Ten feet away, just off the trail, sat a fat raccoon. It hissed. Bitsy barked.

"They aren't usually out in the daytime, are they?" Marty asked.

"Night scavengers. Maybe Bitsy woke him up."

"Not rabid, is it?"

"Doubt it." Digger stooped and snapped her fingers. "Come here, Boy."

Bitsy backed up, slowly.

"Rabid ones usually stumble around, and maybe drool. This guy looks as if he has all his faculties. He just feels threatened."

Bitsy sidled up to Marty, who leaned down to pet him.

"Hey, who feeds you?"

Marty stood. "We men have to stick together. Let's keep walking."

Bitsy looked back several times, and finally seemed persuaded the raccoon would not join their hiking party. He bounded ahead, barking at some likely imaginary movement just off the path.

Marty bent over, picked up a stone, and tossed it at an abandoned bird's nest above them. "I want to come back with my camera."

"Won't be easy to get good shots with all the trees around the cottage."

"How did anyone get to that place, or the larger house?"

"We're above the east side of Maple Grove. If you leave town from the west, an old state road comes up to the house." Digger paused. "I think there used to be an unpaved driveway that came back to the cottage. You can see the trees aren't as tall toward the front of the cottage."

"What happened to the daughter who lived there?"

"Supposedly she ran off with some guy she just met."

"Never came back?"

Digger shook her head. "I don't know all the details. It was maybe twelve years ago or more. I was about twelve or thirteen. You could..." She stopped herself before she said, "Ask Uncle Benjamin."

"I could what?"

"There must be some old articles in the *Maple Grove News*."

"Maybe I'll go down to the historical society to read them."

"Didn't you say the paper is close to digitizing all the back issues? You can read them at your desk."

He nodded. "Yep. But when you search for a topic, it brings up only those articles. I like the microfilm at the society. You get the whole page."

"What difference does it make?"

He shrugged. "I like to see what else was going on at the time. Like when I was looking for articles on the Underground Railroad in the area. You know, to try to help Holly. If a paper mentioned the hunt for someone fleeing slavery, the same page might have a piece on the literal railroad being used for Union supplies, or who was visiting whom in town."

Digger kicked the skin of a large snake from the path into the brush. It had been on Marty's side of the path on the way up, and he hadn't seemed to notice it.

"What are you...gross."

Digger grinned. "City boy. Holly asked me to help find her Western Maryland ancestors, but I'm glad to know she enlisted you, too."

"Huh. Thought she would have told you."

Digger thought her business partner would have let her know that, too, but Holly had talked to a lot of people about her quest. Marty and Digger seemed to be the only two actually working on it.

She changed the subject. "How do those social announcements relate to the Underground Railroad?"

"My theory is that those local visits could have been a good way to transport an escaped slave from one house to another."

"Did you find anything that said those visits really did help transport people?"

"Not really, but Holly wants me to keep hunting, in general. Maybe I'll come up with some connections to her Barton family or people who married into it."

"I feel almost guilty, sometimes. My white grandparents are easy to trace back for several generations. Holly's slave ancestors were numbers on a census, not names."

"I've never gotten into that stuff. When was the first Garrett County Census done?"

"First federal census was 1790, but Garrett County was part of Allegany then. It had 4,800 people and 258 were Black slaves, but probably only a few hundred people, if that, lived in what's now Garrett County."

"Aren't you the walking encyclopedia."

Digger tapped the side of her head. "History major, remember? Anyway, have you had much luck?"

"Not yet. She wants to know who that second great grandmother was, her great grandmother's mother on her mom's side. I honestly don't see how we'll find out." Marty shot her a sideways glance. "Not like we can question her ghost."

Digger's heart beat faster. "I wonder if ghosts remember everything about their pasts?"

"Maybe you can find out."

That comment marked the first time Marty had acknowledged even the possibility that Digger might be the medium for an ornery ghost. She wasn't sure she wanted to continue the topic. At least, not now. "There's a book about ghost towns of the Upper Potomac River. We could visit a couple and see if we meet any."

Marty's tone was flat. "We could."

He had given her an opening and she hadn't taken it. Why not?

They walked to the trailhead where Digger had parked her Jeep. Usually, Digger would say it was as easy to be quiet with Marty as it was to talk. Not this time.

AT THE ANCESTRAL SANCTUARY, Bitsy bounded out of the Jeep and headed for the porch. Digger got out more slowly. "You coming in for supper? Saturday night's leftovers, and I have lasagna and pulled pork."

Marty leaned on the hood of the car and tossed her keys back to her. "I think I'm going to work on a story."

When Digger looked surprised, he added, "I want to hike back up there with a camera tomorrow, so I need to do some work tonight. Want to come?"

From the front porch, behind her, Uncle Benjamin called, *"Make him come in. You won't warm up the pork if he doesn't, and I want to practice smelling it."*

Digger started, but held Marty's gaze. "If it isn't any colder. I'm stiff from hiking in forty-five degree weather."

He grinned. "Wimp. I'll call you before I go to bed."

She waved as he pulled away in his Toyota, and started for the porch. "No surprises, remember?"

Uncle Benjamin made a palms-up shrug. *"Sorry. I thought you saw me on the porch. Got bored waiting for you."*

Digger knew how hard it was for Uncle Benjamin to be limited to either the Ancestral Sanctuary property or wherever she went. True that his pale version of himself could float through walls, but he couldn't make anything move. The one time he'd summoned the strength, or whatever you called it, to push her out of danger, he could barely stand for ages.

She grinned. His ability to transform into any clothes he once wore or anything he saw elsewhere led to some interesting apparel combinations. Today he wore the baseball uniform of a Baltimore Oriole. "I thought you liked the Pittsburgh Pirates best."

"The season's about to start. I feel like I should support a Maryland team." He pounded one hand into a mitt. *"Too bad you can't play catch with me."*

"Spring training underway?"

"Yeah, and this is the Orioles' old uniform." He switched to his favorite red sweater vest over a yellow oxford shirt that had frayed cuffs. His khaki trousers had a tear near the bottom of one leg. He once told Digger that it ripped during a battle with a hedge trimmer, but she'd never asked him what one was doing at his ankle.

Digger pointed to the front door. "Let's head inside."

"Sure. Sorry I startled you." He floated through the door while she unlocked it.

"It's okay. Where's Ragdoll?" The very furry cat rarely left his side. She seemed to sense his presence.

"We were in my son's rooms in the attic. I like to look out that round window."

Digger entered the front hallway. "Watching for me from Franklin's apartment, were you?"

"What are we doing tomorrow?"

Digger had promised Uncle Benjamin she would spend time with him on the Internet on their joint hobby, family history research. "How would you like to take a hike with us?"

"You're going out again?"

"Marty had never been up to The Knob, and he was intrigued by that boarded-up cottage just off the trail." She hung her jacket on the hall coat tree. "He wants to go back with his camera."

Uncle Benjamin floated ahead of her. *"I would have thought that place fell apart by now."*

"It's boarded up pretty tight, and the roof looks intact."

"Old Man Halloway thought his daughter and granddaughter would come back. She supposedly left because he wouldn't increase her monthly allowance."

"Where'd they go?"

"Don't know. You remember it, don't you?"

"I think it was my last year of middle school. I don't remember people talking about it a lot."

"They sent postcards for a while, then nothing. Guess Halloway's daughter found somebody to shack up with."

Digger smiled to herself as she walked past the large living room on her right and the dining room just past it, into the kitchen. Uncle Benjamin's language was becoming more like a teenager's. "What happened to the granddaughter? Was she young?"

"About eight or nine. That was the really sad part. Have to hope she had a happy life."

She opened the fridge and took out the leftover lasagna. "Anyway, you can come if you behave yourself. You can't butt into our conversations."

"I never butt in. I add fascinating details."

CHAPTER TWO

DIGGER SPENT MUCH OF SATURDAY evening poring over books about Garrett County history and searching articles on the Internet. She had promised Holly she'd help her figure out who her great, great grandmother was, but didn't see how she could.

Uncle Benjamin had worked on the Browning family history for decades, and even he had a couple evasive ancestors, mostly women whose maiden names weren't known.

"You know what you need to do? You should write an article about the Underground Railroad in this area."

Digger looked at Uncle Benjamin. "There isn't a lot on that, is there? Supposedly only a few houses were stations on the railway."

"That's kind of my point."

She considered the suggestion. "It's a good idea, but I want to focus on Holly's family first."

"There were a number of free Black families in the 1860 Census. And, of course, 1870 and after. That's the timeframe she thinks she's looking at, right?"

"Yes, but she doesn't know whether her great, great grandmother was a free person or slave."

"You know you have to look back from what she knows for sure. When can she first find her ancestors on the census?"

"Mmm. In 1870, for some of them. Before that, it would only have the owners' names, and then ages and sex of the slaves."

"Right, but if you look at the 1850 and 1860 Censuses, write down the names of the owners. Sometimes freed slaves adopted those names. Allegany County, of course. Garrett wasn't formed until 1872."

Digger sighed. "I guess I find it all so deplorable I haven't worked on it as much as I should."

"But Holly's your friend, so you'll do it. Even if it does lead you to her ornery grandmother."

Digger smiled. "You just crossed swords with Audrey Washington because she argued with you sometimes at the historical society."

"That woman wanted to conduct historical society meetings even if I was in charge." His eyebrows went up and he grinned. "And that brings me back to the Underground Railroad."

"How so? Oh, conduct, conductors, railroad."

"Right. It wasn't just white people who helped slaves escape to Pennsylvania. You should look for names of Black folks."

"Because maybe her ancestors helped other slaves escape?"

"Or provided help to travelers. At least worth looking at. Maybe some of the Western Maryland historical libraries have

letters or diaries -- enough that you could piece things together."

"Sounds like a job for a man with a lot of time on his hands."

"Could be, but somebody'd have to take him to those libraries, or bring home some material."

"I see your ulterior motive now."

"I could stay here some days and work on it. If I had the right books to dive into."

Digger smiled. He couldn't turn pages, but somehow he could plunge into books and look around. "A lot of the material is online, or at least indexed online. I can't check out old reference items, but I'll look for some and make copies for you."

"An efficient young woman could get on that by Monday, when she goes into town to work."

"Okay. The efficient woman hears you. I want to get back to the census data."

Though all of the census data was on Ancestry, Digger had paper copies of the 1850-1870 Allegany County and the 1880 Garrett County Censuses. In 1850, Maple Grove had a smattering of families in the area.

Digger knew from local history accounts that the town had grown around a grain mill and a blacksmith shop, two essential businesses on the frontier. In rapid succession a dry good store, two churches, and a lumber mill followed.

Small farms surrounded the growing town. The rocky terrain and short growing season meant agriculture had never produced much more than food needed for people in the area. Until the twentieth century, anyway.

Digger looked for White families named Washington in 1850 and 1860 and found two, each of which had very few slaves. By current roads, the two families were roughly three miles apart, and there was no indication that they were blood relations.

By 1870, there were also three Black families with the Washington name in the same area. Digger didn't like to jump to conclusions, but the ages of the children and adults in the three new families correlated to those of the slaves in the 1860 Census – plus some new children under ten years of age.

She'd never heard Holly say where she thought the Washington name came from. She likely didn't know, but Digger would ask her on Monday.

MARTY CALLED SUNDAY MORNING to say he would head back to The Knob about eleven. "The sun should give at least a little more warmth mid-day. You coming?"

Digger had made the trek many times, but she was less interested in the hike and cottage than who she'd be walking with. "Sure. Meet in that small parking lot at the trailhead?"

"I could swing by and get you."

Digger thought for a few seconds. "No, I need to stop in town to get groceries afterwards. I'll meet you in the lot."

"I thought this guy you know might take you to the Coffee Engine after the hike."

She laughed. "Work's been so busy I have three loads of laundry and a bunch of branches to stack near the burn barrel."

The first spring rainstorm had littered the Ancestral Sanctuary's lawn and vegetable garden with all the dead limbs the trees had held onto over the winter.

"I should be insulted."

"How about grabbing a bite after work Monday?"

"Sounds like a plan. I'll see you in the lot at eleven."

Digger glanced at the clock on the counter microwave. Nine AM. Plenty of time to throw in some laundry and grab at least one batch of sticks and branches before she left.

She turned to find Uncle Benjamin sitting cross-legged on the red, Formica-topped kitchen table, his favorite spot. "I'd say I didn't hear you come in, but I never do."

"If you're taking your own car, it'll be easier for me to come on the hike."

"Will you walk ahead or behind us, and not offer commentary?"

He adopted an expression of feigned affront. *"Anyone else would value my skills as a tour guide."*

"Anyone else would know not to interrupt other people's conversations."

Ragdoll hopped onto the table and settled in next to him. Digger felt certain the cat strongly sensed his presence. Bitsy was sometimes confused if Uncle Benjamin passed near him, but Ragdoll followed him around just as she did when he was alive.

He petted her, which the cat never acknowledged. Digger wasn't sure if it was typical feline aloofness or if she couldn't tell he touched her.

Uncle Benjamin looked to Digger. *"I heard you and Holly talking about remodeling Aunt Clara's kitchen."*

She took in the cabinets and worn countertops, installed when the kitchen was 'modernized' in the 1940s. "It's dated, and I'd like a dishwasher…"

He waved a hand. *"I meant to do it the last few years. Lots of unused space, and the floor's worn."*

Digger waited. She knew he had a point. Old farm-style kitchens generally served as a family's main eating space, and had a lot of open area, meant to hold a large table and chairs. She wanted to put counters on an additional wall and install an island.

"Any chance you'll leave my table?"

She smiled. "You don't want me to donate it to the historical society?"

He grunted. *"Audrey wouldn't let you bring it through the door."*

"I'm kidding. I'll take out the leaf and probably have the metal trim refinished." She pointed toward the wall that abutted the dining room. "It'll go right there. New chairs, though."

Uncle Benjamin stroked Ragdoll again. *"Hear that? We aren't being evicted."*

DIGGER WAVED AS SHE got out of her Jeep in the parking lot below The Knob.

Uncle Benjamin – sporting hiking boots, shorts, and a battered hat and fishing vest – floated ahead as she moved toward Marty. *"I'll give him a smooch as I go by."*

Without moving her lips, she said, "Don't you dare." She wouldn't be able to keep a straight face. It was hard enough not to laugh at Uncle Benjamin's skinny legs in high-end hiking boots.

Marty leaned into his car and took his camera off the front seat. As he locked the door, he called, "Where's Bitsy?"

"I took her out right before I left. She's good for a few hours." She fell into step beside him as they started toward the wide trail. "She'd be a distraction if you wanted to take some serious pictures."

"Good point." Marty took her hand. "How come you didn't bring your camera?"

"Probably not something Holly and I would use in any promotional ads we design. Not a good example of the housing stock if the Chamber of Commerce is trying to attract new businesses."

"I see your point. The historical society wasn't open, so I went into the newspaper's archives last night."

"You went to your office?"

He shook his head. "We reporters have secret codes to get into the computer system remotely."

"Funny. You read about the cottage?"

"More specifically, the disappearance of the woman and her child twelve years ago."

"I remembered the family name. Halloway, I think."

From ahead, Uncle Benjamin's voice floated to them. *"You should give me credit."*

"Yep. Hamil Halloway. Odd name."

"What was the daughter's name?"

"She was, or I suppose still could be, Samantha, and the child was Cherry."

"Was her name still Halloway?"

"It seems so. She and the little girl lived alone in the cottage. None of the articles mentioned a husband or boyfriend."

Digger let go of his hand to snap a branch that hung over the edge of the path. "If you really get into it, I could check some of the genealogy websites for marriages or anything else that relates to her."

"I thought they only had information on dead people."

"You could tell him about dead people you know."

"Some public records are there, like marriages."

"That'd be good. What relatively little I found made it sound like they didn't do a real thorough search for her."

"What do you mean?"

"Her father made appeals, the sheriff had signs and they posted them throughout the county. Local TV picked up on it. But there was no big canvass of the woods or any large, general search."

"They thought she ran away?" Digger asked.

"I picked up that idea. People who talked about seeing her the last day she was around said she seemed cheerful, happier than usual. None of the traditional signs of foul play, as the cops say."

"So they think she left on her own."

"Yep. She didn't take a lot with her, but enough that it seemed she packed an overnight bag, or something similar. For herself and her daughter."

"That poor family."

"Yeah, her father offered a reward and put ads in our paper and some others."

Digger thought for a moment. "So, your interest in the cottage isn't solely architectural?"

He grinned. "You never know, she could turn up. I'll have good photos of the cottage before they take the boards off the windows."

They concentrated on the uphill climb for a minute.

Uncle Benjamin came back toward them. *"Slowpokes. I'll beat you up there by a longshot."*

Digger ignored him and jutted her chin forward. "The cottage is just ahead, in the trees on the left."

"Huh. Now I get why I didn't see it on the way up last time. When you're walking up, those fallen logs kind of draw your attention." Marty took his camera strap off his shoulder.

Digger glanced at the two logs, which sat across one another, like a giant X. "Tic tac toe."

"Yep." Marty stopped and looked down through his camera's screen. "Better lighting out here, but I guess the cottage won't move onto the path."

A laugh came from behind them, and a man's voice said, "I've been trying to get my wife to let me peer into that cottage. She says there's probably poison ivy."

They turned. A couple of perhaps thirty approached, with a baby forward facing in a harness on the man's chest. The woman's bright red, floppy hat, would be a beacon for bird droppings.

Marty grinned. "My wife has given me permission to take pictures."

Uncle Benjamin peered from behind Marty's shoulder. *"That's a good one."*

Digger forced a smile. "Actually, he tends to ask forgiveness rather than permission."

The two people stopped a few feet from them. Digger recognized the curly-haired man, and he cocked his head at her. "Do you work with Holly Barton?"

She smiled. "I do. Digger Browning." In the post-COVID tradition, she did a four-fingered wave.

"And I'm Marty Hofstedder." He bent down and scrunched his nose at the baby.

"Oh, sure," the woman said. "We haven't met, but I know your faces from around town. I'm Regina and this is Tyler. We just bought the laundromat downtown."

Marty stood. "Duds 'n Suds. I saw you bought an ad about taking over the place. I plan to come by next week to talk to you guys."

Tyler grinned and nodded to Digger. "Great. We changed the name to that because of the ad campaign Holly designed for the last owners, just before they sold to us."

She'd have to remember to tell Holly. They'd both worked on the ads, but the fun tagline had come from her partner. "How's business?"

"Good. We're closed Monday and Tuesday," Regina said. "Then we can have a grand reopening on Wednesday."

Tyler grinned. "We're having the place painted Monday and bringing in a bunch of rolling laundry carts customers can use. Then we can raise the prices a little."

Regina slapped him playfully on the arm. "You aren't supposed to say stuff like that."

"I promise not to mention your Machiavellian tendencies in an article," Marty said.

The baby fidgeted and whimpered. Regina ruffled his hair. "We have to keep our little guy moving."

Digger and Marty stood to one side of the path so they could pass.

"What's the baby's name?" she asked.

"Doogie," Regina said.

"Douglas," Tyler added. "Doogie could get you a punch on the playground."

They laughed and walked past, heading for The Knob.

"It'll be all over town that you two eloped." Uncle Benjamin turned to follow the couple.

They let Regina and Tyler get out of earshot.

Digger pretended to scowl deeply. "Your wife?"

Marty grinned. "It isn't a formal proposal."

She rolled her eyes. "Come on. Let's get your pictures."

For the next ten minutes, Marty took photos of the cottage from several angles and distances. Getting an image of the entire cottage was tough because of trees and the variegated lighting that poked through them.

Digger kept moving around and finally found a good spot. "Come over here. If I hold back this branch you can get a better shot."

Marty tromped over. "My feet are turning into ice clods."

From the path, Uncle Benjamin called, *"Wimp."*

Digger grinned. "You're almost done, aren't you?" She put her foot on a log to steady herself while she reached above her head.

Marty's back was to her. "Yeah, I want to get a couple more of…"

A hissing noise told them they had passed too close to the raccoon. Digger looked behind her as she pulled back the branch. "Hello, Mr. Bandit. We'll be gone soon."

Marty kept peering through his lens.

The raccoon stood on his hind legs and hissed again, more gutturally this time.

"Oh my God!" Uncle Benjamin rushed toward them.

"What?" She almost let go of the branch and Marty ducked.

"Is it rabid? Are you hurt?"

She tried not to show she was breathing harder. "Sorry. It moved and startled me, that's all."

"Okay. I like my eyesight." He brought the camera into position again.

Digger's eyes traveled down the path, following Uncle Benjamin as he ran toward her car. He appeared to be cradling something in his arms, and it looked a lot bigger than a solid raccoon.

CHAPTER THREE

DIGGER HELD ONTO THE branch but turned her head to follow Uncle Benjamin's progress. His transparent image faded among the trees and then vanished from her sight. Marty, eyes on the cottage and his camera, didn't pay attention to her.

The raccoon had dropped to all fours and waddled onto the path. He seemed to stare in the direction Uncle Benjamin had run.

Her thoughts raced. While her uncle had to stay at the Ancestral Sanctuary or with her, nothing in the theoretical ghost handbook said he had to be within a certain distance.

Digger turned toward Marty again, to find him staring at her.

"What is it? You look like you're going to throw up or something."

She forced a smile. "I'll try to miss your shoes. I thought I heard someone on the path behind us. Guess it was my imagination."

He removed the camera strap from around his neck. "Hold onto my camera for a minute."

She took it. "How much can I get for this at a pawn shop?"

"Funny." He pointed to his right. "I think I can climb a few feet up that tree. I'd like to get a couple shots from a higher angle." He started toward the tree.

How long did she have to stay by the cottage? Surely Marty had enough pictures. She told herself to relax. It wasn't as if Uncle Benjamin could trip and kill himself.

Marty stood beneath the white pine and reached up to pull on a low-hanging branch. "Feels sturdy enough." He grabbed for that branch with his left hand and grasped another two feet from it with his right.

Digger stood still as he hefted himself up to the lower of the two branches and lifted one leg over it. He leaned against the tree trunk and reached down to her.

"I think I can stay balanced enough to get good shots."

She moved the few feet to him and handed him the camera. "Steady up there."

Marty didn't look down. "Thanks." He brought the camera to his face and pressed a button so the view screen popped out. For several seconds he looked at it, then at the cottage, then back to the view finder. He began snapping pictures moving the camera and his head slightly after every couple of snaps.

After less than half-a-minute, voices came toward them from the direction of The Knob. Since it was April, there were fewer people hiking than later in the spring. It had to be Regina and Tyler. Absurdly, Digger wondered if the young couple and their baby would get to Uncle Benjamin before she did.

Above her, Marty called, "Take the camera, will you?"

Digger reached up, took it, and quickly stepped back. Marty half jumped and half fell out of the tree, but landed on his feet. "Got a few good shots, I think."

"And you didn't break a leg." Digger feigned a chill and rubbed her upper arms. "Kind of cool down here on the ground. Did you get enough pictures?"

"For now." The laughter from Regina and Tyler came closer. "Hey, I'll see if they want a picture of them and the baby."

"Great idea." Digger walked toward the path, a few paces behind him. Scurrying sounds nearby drew her gaze, and she saw the raccoon's tail vanish into brush under a pine tree.

She didn't rush to catch up, she needed time to think. But she also didn't want to dawdle. She wanted Marty to take the photo so Regina, Tyler, and little Doogie could walk ahead of them.

She drew closer to the group as Tyler put his arm around Regina's shoulder and both smiled toward Marty. At the exact time the camera snapped, the baby chortled.

Digger smiled. "Perfect pose."

"I think so, too," Marty patted a pocket. "Damn. I don't have a pen to write your email."

Tyler laughed. "You're easy to find, your name's on the paper's website. I'll send you a note tomorrow and you can get our email from that." They turned to continue down the path.

Marty looked down at Digger.

She sensed a question, so she smiled brightly. "You want to get one of the raccoon?"

Marty looked toward the cottage. "You know where he went?"

"Just kidding. He ducked under a pine." She started walking toward the car.

Marty fell into step. "You still look odd."

"I could have thrown a rock at you when you were in the tree."

"Okay, I'll leave it alone." They walked in silence for almost a minute. "What was it you said you have to do this evening?"

She drew a blank. "Uh, house stuff. Franklin might come up next weekend, so I don't want to have to do this weekend's laundry with next weekend's."

Marty nudged her with his shoulder. "That sounds like the adult equivalent of a high school girl saying she can't go out because she has to wash her hair."

Digger laughed. "It's going to be a busy week. And we did say dinner tomorrow." She squinted as she looked ahead of them. No sign of Uncle Benjamin.

Marty became more serious. "Sometime you're going to have to figure out if we're going to be more than hiking buddies."

"I...know. It's...complicated."

"Are you afraid I'll be like the last jerk you dated?"

"Don't remind me. And no, I'm not. I just have to sort out some stuff."

Marty shifted his camera strap to his other shoulder. "Let me know if you need any help alphabetizing."

"I promise I will." Car doors opened and shut below them. She figured Tyler and Regina had loaded Doogie into the car.

"As long as you don't throw any rocks at me in the meantime."

"I probably won't." A thought occurred to her. "If I did, who would I call when you fell out of the tree? If you broke your arm or something."

"Aren't we morbid. My grandparents I guess, since they live here. I suppose I'd call Franklin if I fell on top of you."

Digger knew his grandparents, Maria and Malcolm Wilson, or the double M's, as Uncle Benjamin had called them. He didn't talk about his parents at all. "Do your parents live in Maryland?"

"Yep. But we aren't close."

"Oh." When he said nothing more, she looked ahead. They had gotten close to the parking lot. Uncle Benjamin stood outside of her Jeep and gestured that Digger should hurry.

"Digger? You're zoning out again."

"Sorry. What was that?"

"You're acting preoccupied again. I asked where you want to eat tomorrow. I'd rather not go to the Coffee Engine for dinner."

"What about that new place on Union Street? They have American and Mexican food."

"Deal." Marty stopped next to his Toyota. "I'll email you a couple of the photos of the cottage. Tell me which one looks the most desolate."

Digger faced him and smiled. She started when Uncle Benjamin appeared behind Marty and pointed to the car. *"Hurry up! We have to get to the Sanctuary."*

She tried to ignore him. "I'll call you after I look at them." She stood on her toes and Marty bent to kiss her.

Uncle Benjamin stood between them and Digger jumped. If Marty hadn't pulled up, she would have knocked him in the chin.

"I'm sorry! I got a shock. Did you feel it?"

Uncle Benjamin ran back to the Jeep.

"Nope." He frowned lightly and kissed her. "Talk to you later."

Digger walked quickly to the Jeep and climbed into the front seat. She tried not to move her lips. "What's the problem? What were you carrying?"

"It's a child, a little ghost girl. She's fading!"

"My God, Uncle Benjamin, who is she?" She started the car and followed Marty's Toyota as he left the lot. He sped up, and she drove more slowly.

"Don't know. I'm not sure she does, either. You have to hurry."

Digger slowed at a sharp curve. "I don't want to end up in the family plot."

She pulled out of the curve and sped up to forty-five miles an hour, much faster than she liked to drive on mountain roads. "Where did you find her?"

"I saw her eyes. She was looking out of a hollow log. You have to go faster!"

Digger drove across the north side of town and then took Crooked Leg Road up the west side of Meadow Mountain. The Ancestral Sanctuary was only a mile away. She eased off the gas as she went around another curve. In a minute, through the leafless trees, the Gardiners' large home loomed on her right, set back from the road.

"We're almost there, little one."

Digger slowed as she got close to the Ancestral Sanctuary's long drive. How would she be able to tell if Uncle Benjamin had lost his marbles? She made a sharp right turn and slowed as she got closer to the house. "Is she still with you?"

In a tone Digger hadn't heard since she was very young, Uncle Benjamin said, *"There you are, sweet girl. We're almost home."*

Home? She wasn't running a rogue's gallery for ghosts.

She stopped in the circle in front of the porch, intending to ask Uncle Benjamin if he needed her to do anything. But before she could say a word, he had jumped through the car door and run into the house.

Ragdoll leapt off the table in front of the living room window as Digger walked quickly up the steps. Before she had her key in the lock, Ragdoll emitted a low-pitched howl, a sound Digger had never heard her make. Could she sense that Uncle Benjamin had brought a stranger into their midst?

She opened the door to see Ragdoll sitting in the foyer, staring up the main staircase. Her fur stood out as if she'd put her tail in a socket.

Bitsy strolled toward her from the kitchen, where he'd likely been lying by his empty food bowl. His tilted head seemed to say Ragdoll's behavior perplexed him. Clearly, he hadn't sensed a ghost child.

Digger debated heading after Uncle Benjamin, but decided she wouldn't be able to help much if she couldn't see his cargo. She patted Bitsy on the head, sidestepped the bewildered cat, and headed to the kitchen. After the chilly air, she just might add wine to some hot tea.

CHAPTER FOUR

MARTY PULLED IN FRONT OF the house where he rented his one-bedroom apartment. The aging Gary Nelson was a reasonable landlord, all the more so because he was so hard of hearing. Marty could play music at a booming level or he could have the elusive Digger over for an evening and Gary would have no clue if they, finally, ended up in bed together.

He'd never met such an intriguing and frustrating woman. She seemed to genuinely like him, but at least once or twice each time he was with her she zoned out. And she kept putting him off. He wasn't sure if telling her she had to decide was a good idea or not. But if she really wasn't interested in more than hikes and dinner, he needed to know.

He let himself into his small unit and for the umpteenth time told himself he needed to get a bigger place. Books spilled from three large bookcases and the living room/dining room combo wasn't big enough for a couch plus a table and chairs. Not if he wanted the TV in the same room as the couch. Which he did.

Usually on a Sunday he'd fix a decent dinner, but tonight he wanted to load the pictures he'd taken today and think about how they might fit into a feature article for the *Maple Grove News*. He opened the kitchen cupboard he always kept stocked with canned food and grabbed some high-end clam chowder. Not a replacement for the crab soup he used to get on the Baltimore waterfront, but a decent substitute.

While it warmed on the narrow stove, he took the card from his camera and loaded it into the laptop. The folder with today's pictures held forty-two shots. If he could have stayed in that tree longer, he'd have ten or twenty more, but better to have gotten down when he did instead of landing on his butt.

He smiled at the one of Regina and Tyler and their little boy, whose name escaped him. As he took pictures of the cottage from varied angles, he'd managed to get a couple of Digger. In profile she had an almost patrician nose. She thought it was too big, he thought it gave her a regal air. The opposite of her personality, which was more in keeping with the faded jeans and cotton-knit sweater she'd worn today.

"Stop thinking about her."

Of the many photos of the cottage, he kept fifteen. The best was the one Digger had set up for him by finding a spot twenty yards from the building and holding back tree branches. He'd taken many pictures of abandoned buildings through the years, but this was the first one that, minus the boards on the windows, probably looked much as it did when its owners left. Put a big pot of geraniums by the front door and a realtor could stake a for sale sign in front of it.

The soup bubbled in the kitchen. He poured a large bowl and grabbed a hunk of the whole-wheat loaf he'd bought yesterday at the Main Street Bakery.

He went to the notes he'd made the day before when he read old articles about Samantha and Cherry Halloway's disappearance. The twelfth anniversary wasn't for a couple weeks, but the following Saturday would have been Cherry's birthday. He did some quick math. She'd be twenty. Not the little girl with large eyes and shoulder-length, wavy hair.

He made a list of people to call over the next two days. Cherry's prior teachers, Samantha's employer (if she worked), and a friend or two. In other update pieces, Hamil Halloway had always refused comment. It wouldn't hurt to try again.

He finished the soup, picked the four best photos, and sent them to Digger to see which she thought was best. Most desolate.

DIGGER WAS NOT SURE OF ghost etiquette when (if?) a new one arrived, so she waited for Uncle Benjamin to call her from upstairs.

"Can you come up here?"

She raised her voice. "On my way." She picked up the glass of white wine she'd poured – hot tea with a splash was not sufficient – and made for the back stairs. She reached the upstairs hall and went to Uncle Benjamin's former bedroom at the far end of it.

He sat on one side of the double bed, cross-legged, staring at the pillow on the other side. When he looked at her, he put his fingers to his lips.

Digger whispered. "How is she?"

"I combed her hair and showed her how she could think about different clothes and she'd be wearing them. She has on a long pink nightgown. She's sleeping."

"And she's, uh, getting better?"

He frowned, but nodded. "Not quite so transparent. Remember how I need to stay here or with you, and that one time you left me I almost faded away?"

"An accident," Digger murmured.

Uncle Benjamin waved a hand. "Sure, sure. "

"But if the cottage was kind of her place, won't bringing her here make her fade more?"

"My guess is she'd been alone so long that she was ready to…" he brought the knuckles of his hands together and pulled them apart, flaring his fingers. *"Sort of poof out."*

She smiled slightly. "That looked more like an explosion to me."

He regarded her, first frowning, then smiling. *"What I'm hoping is that she can be with another ghost and thrive in my space."*

Digger wanted to hold her hands against her head so her brain didn't burst, but she refrained. "That's great. But can we talk?"

Still goo-goo eyed, he said, *"In a minute."*

Digger crossed to the picture window that overlooked the landscaped lawn and garden before they melted into the trees on the four-acre property. She sank into the deep cushions on the Colonial-style rocking chair, leaned her head back against its rounded top, and closed her eyes for a minute, breathing slowly. When she opened them, Uncle Benjamin stared at her intently.

"For a minute, I thought both my girls were sleeping."

Digger forced a smile. "She's lucky you found her. Does she, uh, know where she is now?"

He shook his head. *"She keeps asking about Mommy and Grandpa. I figured she meant Samantha and Halloway, and told her when she woke up, we'd see if we could find them."*

"What? If you take her over there she'll be really confused." Digger shut her eyes for a moment. She was talking about a ghost child as if she were real.

He shrugged. *"Not sure I know what else to do."*

"In the back of the closet in here is that antique porcelain doll Aunt Clara used to have sitting on the washstand, where the colonial pitcher is now. Maybe it will distract her." She stood.

Finding the doll was easy. At Uncle Benjamin's instruction years ago, she had wrapped it in a soft cloth and placed it on a back shelf in the walk-in closet. She sat her wine on Aunt Clara's tall jewelry box and took the doll down and removed the cloth. The rose-colored dress looked as she remembered it, and the petticoat under its skirt made the hem of the skirt circle the doll, inches from her legs.

Digger had initially wondered if the child was a figment of Uncle Benjamin's lonely imagination, but now she tended to believe him. His concern was real, anyway. And the timing couldn't have been more awkward. Would she eventually hear two ghosts if Marty came over for dinner?

She smiled grimly. On the one hand, Uncle Benjamin probably wouldn't want to ride into town with her every day. On the other, how many more ghosts would he drag home? Then she felt guilty. Ghost or not, somebody had to help this confused child.

She picked up her glass and took a gulp of the white wine. When she walked out of the large closet, Uncle Benjamin stood by the window staring at the vegetable garden below, now fallow. She wondered if he thought about how much he had enjoyed planting each spring.

She placed the doll on the bed, hopefully not where the child slept.

"I brought the doll." He didn't turn around. "Uncle Benjamin, we have a lot to talk about."

He turned to face her. "*You sound like you're scolding me.*"

"I'm not. But you're bringing a new person into the house. I can't see her and don't know if she can see me. If something happened to you, would she be here with me, or does she go away?"

He nodded slowly. "*I get it. I don't know much more about this ghost stuff than you do.*"

"What does she look like?"

He smiled and returned to the bed to sit next to her. "*She's tiny for an eight-year old, long brown hair. She reminds me a little of you. Very bright-eyed. She's not too energetic, but maybe she'll be livelier after she feels better.*"

"Okay. Can she see me?"

Uncle Benjamin frowned. "*I'm not sure who she sees besides me.*"

"Did you ask her about the raccoon?"

"*What raccoon?*"

"Both times that Marty and I looked at the cottage, a good-sized one was near where you found her. He seemed...protective, or something."

He looked at the sleeping child. "*She didn't mention an animal.*"

Digger said nothing for almost a minute. The entire time Uncle Benjamin looked at the pillow – the child -- with an adoring expression.

She spoke softly. "You'll have to ask her some questions."

"*What kind? I don't want to upset her.*"

"You don't have to ask her how she died. But is she really Cherry Halloway? Did someone leave her in that log or did she wake up somewhere else and go to the spot near the cottage?"

Uncle Benjamin stood and began to walk across the room, from window to door and back. "*This isn't a cross-examination. She's a little girl.*"

"I know, Uncle Benjamin. But we can't help her if we don't have a clue what's going on with her. What if she doesn't stop fading, as you call it."

He had stopped next to the bed, and now lifted his gaze from the child. "*You're right, of course. I guess I need some time to think.*"

"Sure. You want me to leave you alone for a while?"

"*Would you? I'm not throwing you out, I have to understand all this better.*"

She grinned. "You can't throw me out. You haven't figured out how to move anything without losing all your strength."

"Smart aleck." But he smiled.

Digger walked down the front stairway and peered into the living room. Ragdoll sat in Bitsy's dog bed -- a first -- her eyes fixed across the room, toward the stairway.

"You want some food, Ragdoll? Come to the kitchen." The cat didn't move.

From the kitchen, Bitsy barked once. Digger had forgotten to give him a treat when she came in. She walked through the dining room. Her hand still clutched the glass of wine, and she took a sip before taking a bone-shaped doggy bonbon from the counter jar and tossing it to the floor.

Bitsy pounced and got dog slobber on the floor as he ate.

As he wagged his tail for more, she wiped up the slobber and pointed to the living room. Tail down, he wandered toward Ragdoll.

Digger sat at the kitchen table. She felt pulled in so many directions. How could she talk to Uncle Benjamin about all this in a way that didn't upset him, much less figure out how a little girl fit into the Ancestral Sanctuary? Would she stay? Uncle Benjamin didn't seem to age. Would a child?

If she was the eight-year-old Cherry who vanished twelve years ago, did that mean she and her mother had died near their cottage? And what happened to their bodies?

CHAPTER FIVE

DIGGER TOOK THE LEFTOVER pulled pork from the freezer and rinsed her wine glass. Uncle Benjamin still hadn't come downstairs. She took the smaller of her two crock pots from a cupboard and placed the frozen concoction and some water in it so the pork could thaw in the pot. Then she turned the setting to high.

The house phone rang. For the tenth time, she wished she'd replaced the kitchen wall phone with a newer one with caller ID, but she was saving her money to remodel the kitchen.

"Digger here."

"Marty on this end. Didn't know if you'd check your email soon. I sent you a few photos of the cottage."

"I'll look in a few minutes. What do you hope to do with them?"

Irritation crept into his tone. "Does it matter?"

"I've heard you say you write one way for a feature and another for a news story. Would you use the same kind of picture for both?"

After a two-second beat, he said, "Sorry, that was grouchy. Plus," his tone lightened, "I didn't realize you paid that much attention when I rambled about my writing."

"On a good day."

"It's only two weeks until the twelfth anniversary of their disappearance, and Saturday coming up would have been Cherry's ninth birthday. I'll use those two things for a starting point for an article in Friday's paper."

"Okay. I think earlier you said most forlorn photo."

"Desolate. Forlorn implies emotion. Cottages don't have any."

"Jeez. I'll look at them and let you know. I have to go wash my hair."

He laughed and hung up.

Digger put in a load of laundry, cleaned the downstairs bathroom, and ran the vacuum on the first floor. She loved the Ancestral Sanctuary, but every time she cleaned it, she longed for the tidy bungalow in town that she'd sold after Uncle Benjamin died. Or whatever you called what he did.

As she wrapped its cord around the vacuum handle, Uncle Benjamin came down the main staircase, obviously holding the hand of someone much shorter. He smiled at Digger. *Cherry wanted to meet you, but she never liked the sound of a vacuum.*

When Uncle Benjamin floated or walked into a room, she saw him coming. When he suddenly popped up behind her, Digger figured he had some ability that let him will himself to another part of the house or her office. Either way, she only talked to him when she could see him. Talking to the unseen Cherry would be very different.

"Please tell her I'm happy to meet her. You want to sit in the living room?"

Uncle Benjamin, still holding her hand, crossed the foyer and guided her to the couch. He pointed to the easy chair across from it. *"Have a seat and I'll explain how this works."*

Bitsy came back into the living room. He didn't like vacuums either. But where had Ragdoll gone?

As Digger sat, she had the answer. From under the couch came a low growl, the kind Ragdoll emitted if another animal wandered into her line of sight as she sat in the front window.

Uncle Benjamin straightened and his arm stretched toward the staircase. *"It's okay, Cherry. It's my cat. Ragdoll. I told..."* It appeared Cherry had broken away and run up the steps because he headed that way. *"We'll be back."*

Digger blew out a breath and got on her hands and knees to peer under the couch. Two green eyes stared at her. "Come on, Ragdoll. You're going to have to share your human, or whatever he is, so you better get used to it." She patted the floor. "You want to see Bitsy?"

Bitsy yelped and padded over. Ragdoll hissed, so he stopped to study Digger as she stretched out on her stomach on the floor.

"Come on, wouldn't you rather be in your window than under there?" When Ragdoll only blinked, she stood. "Come on, Bitsy. We'll get her a couple pieces of that soft kitty treat she likes."

Digger brought in three treats and sat one a few inches from the couch. Faster than she could have imagined, a furry paw stretched out and pulled it under the sofa.

"Pretty smart." She sat cross-legged a few feet from the couch. "Come on. You smell these?"

The cat's nose and then head appeared and she meowed at Digger.

Digger stood, showed Ragdoll the treats, and walked to the table in front of the window to deposit them next to the lamp.

Ragdoll emerged, moved quickly toward the window, and hopped lightly onto the table.

"Good. Don't growl at anybody. Or any...whatever." She went to the staircase and called up. "Ragdoll's in her spot by the window." No response. "Nobody will growl. Come see my dog."

Uncle Benjamin's voice drifted down. *"We're on our way."*

Bitsy sat on the floor next to Digger's chair. Less than a minute later, Uncle Benjamin repeated his entrance, clearly holding Cherry's hand.

He smiled at Digger. *"You can talk to her directly. She hears you fine."*

"Hello, Cherry. I hope you're feeling okay."

Uncle Benjamin smiled broadly. *"Much better."* They settled on the couch.

Digger glanced at Ragdoll. For a change, she sat facing the room, but she didn't hiss or growl. Bitsy never seemed to sense when Uncle Benjamin was around, so he just head-butted Digger's knee until she scratched his head.

Uncle Benjamin leaned into the couch. *"She thinks Bitsy is funny. I've explained to Cherry where we found her, and that we brought her to my house so she could be with someone else who could talk to her."*

Digger looked next to Uncle Benjamin. "We're glad you're here, Cherry." When she apparently didn't reply, Digger added, "I think I saw your raccoon friend earlier today…"

Uncle Benjamin turned quickly to the place next to him. *"Okay. Yes. Just fine, I'm sure."* He faced Digger with an almost reproachful expression. *"Can you tell her where you saw Big Eyes?"*

"Big..? Oh, yes. I think near where my uncle found you. I kind of thought the raccoon was…"

"Big Eyes," Uncle Benjamin said.

"I thought Big Eyes was your friend, because he watched when Uncle Benjamin carried you down the trail."

From Uncle Benjamin's expression, Digger knew he was listening to Cherry. After almost a minute, he said, *"Yes, he was her friend. She stayed in the log a lot, and he would make her warm sometimes."* He glanced at Cherry and back to Digger. *"She doesn't understand why I have to repeat what she says."*

"Well, Cherry, I think I can see Uncle Benjamin because I've known him all my life. You and I never met when…before you met Big Eyes. I guess that's why I can't see or hear you."

Uncle Benjamin nodded a few times toward a sofa cushion, and then he looked at Digger. *"I've tried to explain a lot. Thank you for doing a better job."*

Digger grinned. "You're welcome." She thought of Marty's photos of the cottage. "My friend took some pictures of your...of the cottage next to the log. Would you like to see them?"

"She would. She also wants to know why the cat doesn't like her."

"You can tell her that while I get my phone and bring up the pictures." Digger stood and retrieved her phone from the kitchen. She stood there for a minute to open Marty's email and bring up the photos. Though small on her phone, they were clear.

Back in the living room, Uncle Benjamin stood by the window and pointed to Ragdoll, apparently introducing Cherry to the cat. Digger sat in the chair and waited.

A minute later, Uncle Benjamin turned toward her. *"Cherry's already at your left elbow. Tilt the phone to her, would you? OK, she can see the picture.*

A look of consternation crossed Uncle Benjamin's face as he sat on the sofa. *"Okay. Okay. Come sit by me."* Cherry apparently did because he pulled her to him in a one-arm hug.

"She's upset because the cottage used to have flowers by the door and all the windows were open. It looks very sad. And where is her mommy? She wants her mommy."

Digger decided to move to the couch. She sat at the end opposite Uncle Benjamin and Cherry and patted the spot next to her. "I can't see you, Cherry, but you can sit here if you want."

After another thirty seconds of Uncle Benjamin saying comforting words, he said, *"She's moving to sit next to you. She just leaned against your arm."*

Digger felt nothing. "That's nice." She tilted her head in Cherry's direction. "We're sorry your mommy is lost. You used to be lost, and I'm so glad my Uncle Benjamin found you."

Uncle Benjamin gave her a nod of encouragement.

"I'm not sure where to look for your mommy, but I'll see if I can find out anything. I bet she had a lot of friends."

Uncle Benjamin frowned slightly, apparently listening. After a minute, he said, *"Mommy had a lot of friends when Cherry was little, but after the Yeller started coming to see her a lot, the other friends didn't visit very much."*

Digger kept her expression impassive. "I'm sorry to hear that. I hope the Yeller was nice to you and your mommy."

Again a pause, and he said, *"Most of the time, but Grandpa didn't like him. Mommy got mad at Grandpa because he didn't want the Yeller to visit."*

Digger knew her sister would know how to tease information from a child, but she had no idea. She decided not to ask her the kinds of questions a police interrogator would. "I bet you had a lot of friends, too. Who was your best one?"

Uncle Benjamin smiled as he listened to her. *"Her best friend was Christina, but she liked to be called just Tina."* He smiled more. *"Jennifer wanted to be Jennie."* He grew serious. *"Can they come over to play?"*

Digger really wished she hadn't asked about her friends. She thought for a minute. "Do you know why I can't see or hear you, Cherry?"

"My, that's a deep sigh, sweet girl." Uncle Benjamin glanced quickly to Digger and then resumed looking at Cherry. He patted the spot next to him. Cherry apparently moved there.

After a long, silent minute, as he nodded several times, he spoke to Digger. *"She thinks it's because of the hide-and-seek game in the log. Mommy told her to hide there until she came to get Cherry. Cherry fell asleep. When she woke up, there was a little bit of snow on the leaves, and Mommy never found her. She thinks she should have stayed awake. Excuse me, she knows she should have."*

Digger's first thought was that Samantha Halloway knew she and her daughter were in some kind of danger, and she hid Cherry. She stayed in the log until she fell asleep, which surprised Digger. That seemed to be a lot of patience for an eight-year-old. If it snowed, did that mean Cherry froze to death?

Digger cleared her throat. "Sometimes we just get so sleepy we can't stay awake. I get that way, too, especially at night."

"Oh my, that's a big yawn." Uncle Benjamin gave the air next to him a one-arm hug. *"You want to lie down in your bed?"*

Apparently she did, because Uncle Benjamin stood and murmured to Cherry as they made their way up the staircase. Digger said nothing, but wondered which room he had designated as Cherry's.

She sat for a moment, then moved to the other side of the living room. She had kept Uncle Benjamin's desk where he'd had it, on the wall next to the dining room. However, she'd taken his genealogy files off his ancient desktop computer and transferred everything to a laptop, which now sat on the desk. He had fretted that anyone could steal the laptop, but Digger had shown him that all of his files were also stored on Google Drive. And they had passwords, so not just anyone could read them.

She turned on the laptop and went to the word processing program to make notes.

- Samantha Halloway and her father didn't agree about a man who could have been a boyfriend.
- Her friends may not have liked "the Yeller" because they stopped coming to the house as often.
- Samantha probably hid her daughter because she sensed someone wanted to hurt her or them.
- Someone must have, because Samantha didn't return for her.
- Cherry may have frozen to death in a spot that would have made her hard to find later.
- That damn raccoon can see ghosts.

She thought some more and then brought up Marty's photos of the cottage. He had sent four. One was from a distance, the one Digger had helped him take by holding branches out of the way. Three others were closer, from the front and each side. The back faced the path and had more growth around it, probably to disguise the little house somewhat.

As far as she could tell, all showed a desolate setting. The plywood on the windows couldn't have been there long; it had not discolored much. So even after all this time, someone must do more than make sure the roof didn't leak.

Something red caught her eye and she put her nose an inch from the computer screen. An early season cardinal?

The red sweater belonged to an older man among the trees. He leaned forward next to a tall stick or cane, and from his rigid posture, he did not want people taking pictures of the abandoned cottage.

CHAPTER SIX

IF HAMIL HALLOWAY WAS the man in the photo, and he surely was, he still lived in the large house near the cottage. Digger could talk to him. But before she did, she'd like to know more about him. She did a lot for the Maple Grove Historical Society and had never encountered him. At the very least, he had reclusive tendencies.

She wondered what he thought about his daughter's disappearance twelve years ago, and whether he thought she was alive. Did he continue to search for Samantha and Cherry?

Digger could talk to Audrey Washington or Thelma Zorn at the historical society, but any questions she asked would soon be all over town.

Maryann Montgomery's image popped into her head. The very senior citizen had recently moved from Oakland, the county seat, to be closer to her grandson, Sheriff Montgomery, and her nephew and his family.

It would be more natural for a returning resident to ask about a case. Case! She wasn't some detective.

Digger would simply mention seeing the cottage when she and Marty were hiking. Maryann's natural curiosity would take over. Maybe she'd even ask her sheriff grandson. Digger smiled. She thought she could trust Maryann to be sneaky.

The very sharp Maryann would want to know what piqued Digger's curiosity. Somehow, saying she'd met Halloway's granddaughter's ghost didn't sound like a good conversation starter. She'd have to think of something.

After a quick dinner, she called Marty. "I think all the pictures are pretty desolate, but one has a big surprise. Did you spot it yet?"

"Give me a clue."

"Look for something red and call me back." She hung up.

Her phone rang ten minutes later. "You could have told me which picture."

"That would have taken all the fun out of it. Hamil Halloway, you think?"

"Almost have to be. I guess he didn't want me taking pictures. Wonder why he didn't say anything?"

Digger shrugged to herself. "Maybe he could tell we were about to leave. If he had enough money to build his daughter a house on his property, why would he put it so close to a well-traveled path?"

"I can tell you that. You know much of Meadow Mountain is state parkland. There didn't used to be a wide trail there, just a narrow hiking path. When the state decided to widen it for broader use, Halloway protested the proximity to the cottage."

"I can see why he might."

"I came across his dust-up with the parks department people. It turned out whoever built the cottage for him put it seven feet onto state land. They ended up granting him some sort of easement, for twenty-five years, but they wouldn't reroute the path expansion."

Digger thought about that for a moment. "So the cottage was initially more secluded. I bet the only reason there isn't graffiti on it is because it's such a steep hike up there."

After several seconds of silence, Marty asked, "Have you thought any more about what I said?"

"I'm working on it. Are we still on for dinner tomorrow night?"

"Sure. I'll text you. Good night." He hung up.

Digger felt dejected as she climbed into bed two hours later. Uncle Benjamin had found a ghost child, and Marty had more or less put her on notice that she needed to decide if she wanted them to be more than buddies. The two situations seemed to cancel each other out.

AS SHE DROVE TO TOWN Monday morning, Digger thought more about Cherry and what finding her alone meant. She wanted to ask her at least a few more questions. Did she know she was a ghost? Why had she stayed by the cottage for twelve years? Or did she know that much time had passed? Since she wanted to see her friends, probably not.

Selfishly, Digger hoped Samantha Halloway's ghost could be found. Perhaps Cherry could be with her. Digger frowned. Or maybe Samantha would come to the Ancestral Sanctuary. "That's all I need."

She approached the hardware store Uncle Benjamin used to own and turned off Crooked Leg Road toward Main Street. She'd hardly thought about work all weekend. Usually by Monday morning she had at least one fresh idea for garnering more business.

Digger parked behind the building where she and Holly had their second-floor office. She grabbed a folder and her purse and walked toward the front of the building. The spring temperatures meant the yellow cotton-knit sweater she wore could be too warm for the afternoon. But since the mountain temperatures would almost immediately lead to a cool evening, the sweater would be a better choice when she met Marty for dinner.

She had beaten Holly to their business – You Think, We Design. She started the coffee pot and stood at the picture window while it brewed. Their second-floor window offered a tremendous view of the town and its multi-colored buildings.

Across the street, lights came on in the small children's clothing store.

She glanced up and down Main Street, but saw only two people. They walked quickly, probably toward the Coffee Engine. Since Maple Grove sat in a small valley, she also looked beyond the town to the rising mountain behind it. Where there had been only bare branches last week, the trees bore green buds. As usual, the evergreen pines looked the same.

As the coffee finished perking, the first-floor door to the building opened and Holly came rapidly up the stairs. Their office door opened and Digger called, "Coffee's ready, tardy woman."

Holly, breathless, closed the door and took off her deep purple trench coat. "Eight-thirty-one. You never beat me."

"Had a busy weekend, but couldn't sleep." She finished pouring her own coffee and stood away from the counter so Holly could pour hers.

The phone rang and Digger answered. "You Think, We Design." She paused to listen. "Good morning, Abigail."

Holly rolled her eyes. They liked their former colleague from the Western Maryland Ad Agency, but these days a call from her meant her current boss, the Chamber of Commerce's director, wanted them to do something for free.

"I get it," Digger said. "Gene wants us to take pictures at the ribbon cutting for the reopening of Suds and Duds, which we would do anyway. Does he want to pay for a photo for the chamber newsletter?"

She listened for another half-minute. "I'll tell you what. We'll give him three pictures, he can use one." She named a ridiculously low fee and listened again. "I know, I know. But if we don't charge him something he'll keep asking for freebies. Then everyone will expect us to be the town photographers." After another few seconds, she added, "See you over there."

She grinned at Holly. "Poor Abigail. Now she'll have to listen to Gene complain about paying us a pittance."

Holly brought the coffee to her desk, which sat in the middle of the large office. "Same old same old."

Digger sat at her desk, at the wall on the side of the room opposite the picture window. She turned on the computer. "I forgot to tell you that Marty and I ran into Regina and Tyler when we hiked up to The Knob Sunday. They love the ads you did."

"We did. I just heard they'd closed for a time."

"Just for a couple of days. They're repainting. Wednesday will be a grand reopening." Digger would take a few photos for a modern-day archive she and Holly were creating. They rationalized that if they became the go-to place for photos of the town, maybe other towns, too, they could bring in a little money selling the digital copies.

Since they'd lost one of their larger clients a few months ago, the two of them had scrambled to find businesses in and near Maple Grove that needed brochures made, photos for publicity they were doing themselves, or mundane things like business order forms. Anything to keep them afloat.

"Do they still call that big ol' rock Lover's Lane?"

"No, smarty, they took out the stones where people sat. Marty'd never seen it."

Holly started to type something. "Uh huh."

"Did you know the woman who vanished from up there? Samantha Halloway? Marty took pictures of her boarded-up cottage."

"Nope. I think her little girl was in my cousin's class at school. I guess no one ever heard from them again."

"Speaking of people who are hard to find..." Digger waited until Holly looked at her. "I'm learning a lot as I try to find out more about your Washington family ancestors."

"Good. Like what?"

"Uncle Benjamin always said freed slaves sometimes took the family name of their former owner. I found two Washington white families, unrelated I think, near where your Washington ancestors first appeared in 1870."

Holly frowned. "First appeared by name, you mean.'

"Of course. Each of the two White families had a few slaves, and the ages correspond to the Black families I found in 1870."

"My Grandmother Audrey said she heard the family picked that name when they were freed. In honor of George Washington, or something like that."

Digger nodded. "And that could be true. Lots of Black families chose Washington, Lincoln, and Jefferson."

Holly shook her head. "I can't be at all sure if they adopted a name or picked one. For some reason, Grandmother Audrey has never been too interested in her in-laws' history."

"Kind of natural. I didn't realize how little I knew about Aunt Clara's family – Uncle Benjamin's wife – until just last year."

"I guess. I kidded her one time about whether she was hiding something, and she told me to mind my manners."

"She's always felt free to scold me, too. Anyway, for now, if you don't mind, I'm going to research this as if those families that appeared in 1870 had been slaves in the White Washington families. You okay with that?"

"I'm okay with anything that fills in the blanks."

CHAPTER SEVEN

MARTY WASN'T ONE TO admit defeat, but he wasn't coming up with any new information about Samantha and Cherry. He hated to just do a rewrite of earlier updates on their disappearance.

He decided to try Hamil Halloway's phone again. Maybe he hadn't heard the two prior messages and would answer this time.

On the third ring, someone picked up the phone and a man's voice said, "Mr. Hofstedder, I have made it clear through the years that I give no interviews."

Marty plowed ahead. "I won't quote you. I wondered if you still held out hope that you would see them again."

"That sounds like an interview question." The receiver went down with a sharp click.

He stared at his phone for a moment. None of the articles at the time suggested that Samantha had a difficult relationship with her father, but Marty wondered if the reason Halloway never spoke to the media was because they had fought before she left.

He went back to handwritten notes from ten years ago. Earlier ones had not survived a file purge at the *News*, but since then a smarter publisher had realized that the case could become active again. Though probably only if a body were found.

A marginal note listed Rose McCaffery as someone who worked at a dance studio where Cherry had taken lessons. The number listed no longer worked. She likely had a cell phone now. He went to the paper's paid subscription for phone and address listings and came up with a more current number.

Rose answered on the second ring and listened to Marty describe his plans to write about Cherry's upcoming birthday and the anniversary of the disappearance.

After a pause, she said, "She was a sweet little girl, but it was a long time ago. I don't really have anything to add."

"I remember you previously said she was excited about a new dance. I wondered if you remembered who dropped her off or picked her up at your studio. Always her mother?"

After several seconds, Rose blew out a breath. "Usually her mom, occasionally a man I think was her boyfriend, though he could have been just a friend."

"Who was that?"

"Karl Hindberg."

Marty racked his brain. "That's a familiar name but I can't quite place it."

"He runs the library. Quiet now, but back in the day he knew how to have a good time."

"Did Cherry seem to like him?"

Rose said nothing for a moment. "It sounds more like you're investigating a crime than doing an update. Do you know something other people don't?"

"I'm sorry. Reporters can be brash. I hiked near their cottage recently. So peaceful. I can't imagine Samantha leaving it by choice."

"I only knew her as a mother who was happy her daughter liked to dance. It did seem…odd that she never told Cherry they were leaving. I can't imagine that bubbly child would have kept a secret. Even if it was just a weekend trip or something."

"I appreciate you talking to me. I'll let you know if I find anything."

"Hard to imagine after all this time, but I hope you find they're living happy lives someplace else."

He tapped his pencil on his desk as he thought about who to talk to next. Probably Hindberg, but he didn't know much about the man.

He went to Facebook and found Hindberg easily, but little was visible without being his friend on the platform. It showed where he lived and went to high school, which Marty knew, and that he was a librarian. It didn't say specifically where he worked. What little there was spoke of a responsible, even staid, man in his late thirties.

The page did list some of his other friends, including the city's budget manager, Clinton Evans, who Marty was friends with.

Marty went to Evans' page. He had accepted the man's friend request as he did for anyone in Maple Grove. For that reason, his own posts didn't reveal a lot about his personal life, not that it was terribly exciting.

Evans used Facebook to document much of his life, including any party he attended, birthday events, and the town Fourth-of-July parade, where he posed as Abraham Lincoln every year. Tall and rail thin, he fit the role to a T.

More interesting were photos from a high school reunion party two years before. Marty did some quick math. It was the twenty-year reunion, which made Hindberg closer to forty than Marty had thought. Two years or three years older than Samantha, whose class had scheduled their twentieth for the coming June.

Most of the class photos were the typical group shots with women looking terrific in stylish dresses and men, often with a beer in their hands, appearing to care less about how history recorded their progress through life.

Someone named Lou Ferrelli posted a photo of Hindberg standing next to the makeshift bar with a can of Coke. The caption was, "KH with his new brand of Coke." Under it someone wrote "the calmer Karl."

Below that photo someone else had added a picture of a younger Hindberg with a face that appeared to be contorted in rage. Marty noted that Hindberg held a small, triangular flag on a thin dowel, meaning the photo was likely taken at a football game or similar event. In a town the size of Maple Grove, Friday night football was a huge spectator sport, even for adults.

Under the face-of-rage picture were several comments. One said, "Madman at work," and another said, "The quiet Karl is a new brand."

Marty contemplated the photos. There were more comments about the librarian than some others, but he could have a lot of mutual friends with Clinton Evans.

It seemed Hindberg had used cocaine in younger days, but that was hardly unusual. The calm exterior visible today could be very different from his younger self, but that again was true for many people. Interesting that a couple people commented on it.

He wished he could see Hindberg's posts without friending him, but no dice.

Marty decided to give Sheriff Montgomery a chance to weigh in on the upcoming twelfth anniversary of Samantha and her daughter's disappearance.

He cut off Marty mid-sentence. "Nothing has changed in the last few years, Hofstedder. Wish it had."

"Guess the big change is the reporter asking the questions. I moved here to take the place of the guy who wrote the last update, and he didn't fill me in beyond what he wrote."

"Sure, I'll talk to you, but I'm not spoon-feeding you. You read the history?"

"Anything I could find."

Montgomery grunted. "Then you know we told people to keep an eye out for them pretty quickly, because of the little girl. I personally tromped the woods around that cottage."

"Look in the cottage?"

"Got permission from Hamil Halloway. Went through it ourselves and with him. His only comment was it looked neater than usual. Looked like they just went out for breakfast."

"No boyfriend she fought with, anything like that?"

"No. Find another angle." They talked for five more minutes, and all Marty learned was that Montgomery was fairly new with the Sheriff Department at that time and he was frustrated that none of the tips that came in were more than people thinking they'd seen the pair. "No rhyme or reason to any sightings. If people really see somebody, there's usually a progression. Like see 'em in Maryland one day, Virginia the next, Georgia after that. But nothing."

"Okay, Marty began, "I appreciate..."

"Listen, Hofstedder, you're from Baltimore. This is Maple Grove. Don't sensationalize the daylights out of this."

"Somebody knows something, Sheriff."

"I don't doubt it." Montgomery hung up.

WHEN HOLLY WENT TO THE Coffee Engine to grab a sandwich for lunch, Digger sent an email to Franklin. She should have called him yesterday, but hadn't thought to do it, and she never called him during his workday in DC.

"Hello cuz. Marty and I walked up the mountain to The Knob this weekend, and he had some questions about that abandoned cottage. Was Samantha Halloway in your high school class? I don't remember much about all of it except that she left with her daughter and never came back."

Digger ate her apple and a granola bar. The Internet in the office was a lot faster than at the Ancestral Sanctuary, so she did a Google search for Samantha Halloway. No article from the time she disappeared came up, but one that Marty's predecessor wrote several years ago did surface.

There had been no Amber Alert because no one offered clear information that Cherry had left against her will or was in danger. Simply being away with a parent, even one who exercised questionable judgment, did not count as being a child in imminent peril.

The article noted that at the time there had been no information on what they wore, but that family members did believe that Cherry had taken her Barbie doll.

The earlier piece also confirmed what Uncle Benjamin had said about her father receiving a few postcards from her, and gave the date of the disappearance as late in October. In the mountains, that could easily mean winter weather. She went to the weather.gov site and learned the temperature that night dropped to twenty-eight degrees. Certainly low enough for a small child to freeze to death.

Near the end of the article was a link to the flyer circulated at the time of their disappearance. A relaxed-looking Samantha Halloway wore a deep maroon dress – or blouse, anyway – with a short gold necklace. Highlighted hair touched her shoulders in a gentle wave, and she smiled broadly.

Cherry's wavy hair had been styled for what must have been a formal portrait, and a silver barrette kept it from spilling onto her forehead. She smiled brightly. Digger wondered if the picture had been a gift for Samantha's parents.

Wording on the flyer named them and stressed that family members "sought information" on the pair.

While there was no evidence that they were in danger the Sheriff Department wanted to "establish their location." The department's phone number and website were provided, but nothing else.

Digger stared at the flyer for another moment. No mention of how to help search or where they were last seen. Everything about the disappearance seemed so sterile.

She closed the screen as Holly returned from the Coffee Engine, and glanced at an email that popped up.

Franklin had responded. "Not sure I ever talked to her. She was a year behind me, but you know how small the high school is. I remember she was one of two girls, maybe three, who sat at a table at the back of the cafeteria. I don't think anyone bothered them, they just liked to be by themselves. One of the other girls might have been Maybelle. You aren't digging into something that's better left buried, so to speak, are you?"

CHAPTER EIGHT

DIGGER LEFT WORK A FEW minutes early Monday evening so she could rush home to let Bitsy do his business. He didn't like that she was leaving again, so she promised to bring him some leftovers.

At the restaurant, Digger shut her menu before Marty finished scanning the Los Amigos' offerings. He folded his menu and nodded to get the server's attention. "You decided so quickly. Have you been here a lot?"

"No, but I liked the chicken fajita, so why try anything new?"

"New opportunities for your stomach? You might like the burritos? Maybe…"

"Okay, I'll take a bite of whatever you get, and I might let you have a taste of mine."

He wiggled his eyebrows, which made his glasses slide down his nose.

She ignored his supposed humor. "You know, there's a place in Frostburg where you could get new frames."

"You sound like my grandmother." He shrugged. "I need a new prescription. I'll get it done one of these days."

The server brought a bowl of corn chips and salsa after she took their order, and Digger dug in. She hadn't had anything since the granola bar. "Did you find any more articles about Samantha Halloway?"

He regarded her for a couple of seconds. "I don't get it, Digger. You knew that old cottage was there all this time. Why the sudden interest in what happened to Samantha and her daughter?"

She thought for a moment. She couldn't say, "Because Cherry Halloway is a ghost living in my house." Instead, she said, "I guess it hit me when we were up there that they were here one day and gone the next. And it doesn't seem that anyone put a lot of effort into seeing what happened to them."

Marty leaned back in his chair. "Sheriff Montgomery might disagree."

"What did they do?"

"He didn't catch the initial call, but he participated in some of the search." Marty held up a hand when Digger appeared about to interrupt him. "I didn't say there were intense searches. But they did talk to all of her friends and the teachers at her daughter's school. They asked police locally and in Ocean City to look for her."

"Ocean City, Maryland or New Jersey?"

"Maryland. Apparently, she liked to go there every summer. Only place outside of the county she traveled to, even if it was only a couple times a year."

Digger frowned. "I don't remember Franklin ever mentioning the search."

"Wouldn't he have been in college by then?"

"Probably first year of law school. So, at Georgetown University."

"So he was probably away at the time. I don't mind thinking it through with you, but are you planning on doing something?"

She shook her head slowly. "That little girl was eight. What if she's alive somewhere in a lousy home environment? She has a grandfather who'd probably help her."

His eyes narrowed. "You talk about her as if she's a child. She's twenty. She could have kids of her own."

Digger smiled. "I guess she could. I should drop it."

But she wouldn't.

HOLLY'S FAMILY NAMES SWIRLED in Digger's brain as she spread research material on the dining room table Monday evening. She owed it to her friend to pay more attention to an issue so close to her heart.

A meow from the living room drew her attention. "Ragdoll?"

She was not on the table in front of the window that overlooked the porch. Not near the fireplace, another favorite spot, or on the couch. She wasn't allowed on the couch – as if she could be trained – and Digger hadn't heard the thump of the cat jumping to the floor just before she walked into the room.

Another meow. Ragdoll stuck her head out from under the couch.

"What are you doing under there?"

Uncle Benjamin's voice came from the hallway, his expression troubled. *"I think Cherry chases her. For fun, not to hurt her, but Ragdoll doesn't like it."*

"I guess that confirms that Ragdoll can sense her, too." Digger took in his outfit. In the house he usually wore some of his former clothing – comfortable knit or flannel shirts, khaki pants, or lightweight jeans. Today he had on an outfit reminiscent of the Good Witch in *The Wizard of Oz.* Lots of chiffon and petticoats.

"Where's your wand?"

"Very funny. We're playing dress-up and hide and seek."

Digger grinned. "You never played dress-up with me."

He frowned. *"I think she went back to Clara's closet. I have to find her."* As he floated up the main staircase, he added, *"You were a tomboy."*

"Yes, I was." She stooped to pet Ragdoll. "Interesting that you know she's chasing you. I'm sorry, Girl."

Ragdoll pulled her head back under the couch. Bitsy had been lying on the hearth, and his ears pricked up at the chance to have a head rub.

"You're okay, Boy. Why don't you sit by Ragdoll?"

Not at all his custom, he did as she said. After stretching he came over and plopped in front of the couch. Ragdoll put one paw out and quickly pulled it back. Digger knew she wanted Bitsy to put his nose under the couch. She wouldn't scratch him, but she'd bop his nose.

Digger went back to looking for Holly's elusive great, great grandmother. Holly had made her own family tree on Ancestry.com, but Digger had one of the Barton and Washington families that she created and kept private.

She wanted to be able to save information that might or might not be related to the search. If she worked in Holly's tree, when Holly went back to it, she might think Digger had made a find, when it was really just a hint. No sense getting her hopes up.

Digger also had access to Holly's tree so she could keep track of hints that resulted from Holly's DNA test. Holly had initially been excited if someone contacted her about a possible link.

However, most messages she received ended up being wishful thinking on the sender's part, and she got frustrated. Her request to Digger was to "separate the diamonds from the coal." Digger didn't bother to tell her that while diamonds were occasionally found when digging for coal in the mountains, the idea that they were formed with it had been debunked.

She had added Holly's Barton and Washington parents, grandparents, and great-grandparents to the tree she created. She added information on their siblings when she could find it. Sometimes a sibling of a grandparent would have more information than the grandparents themselves, and Digger could work back a generation from there.

Holly's Grandmother Audrey Washington's husband was the late Daniel Washington. Her great grandfather was Jeremiah Washington. Digger made the tentative assumption that Holly's great, great grandfather was also named Washington. But since the names of some former slaves were in flux just after the Civil War, she would need to find something that said that.

She studied what she had. Great Grandfather Jeremiah Washington was born in 1868, and his wife Ruth (whose maiden name was not yet known), in 1878. So, both after slavery ended.

Holly's Grandfather Daniel thought his father's ancestors had lived on the west side of Meadow Mountain, but he had never heard Jeremiah and his wife Ruth talk much about Jeremiah's parents. He told Holly he'd probably been told some things, but long since forgotten them. And Daniel had died a few years ago, so Holly couldn't prod his memory.

It surprised Digger somewhat that Audrey, so active in the historical society, hadn't dug into her husband's ancestors much. But a lot of people had little interest in their in-laws' history.

If Jeremiah Washington was two years old in 1870, his parents and any siblings should be on the 1870 Census for Allegany County. But where? For now, she would assume his parents had probably been slaves rather than a free Black family in earlier years, but that couldn't be certain.

Usually when Digger did a tree on Ancestry, it provided suggestions – a lot of them – for each person's life progression and that of their parents and siblings. And so on. She did not accept these as fact unless they coincided with other information.

Since her search for Holly was based on local families, she would normally go to the Maple Grove Historical Society for verification, or at least support. In the last couple of decades more material on Black families was being gathered. Sources weren't necessarily Baptismal or school records for families who weren't allowed go to church or school.

Still, some family Bibles were donated, or at least the family pages photocopied. Several high school projects had transcribed oral histories. With roughly 300 Black people out of about 29,000, there wasn't a lot of data to collect.

Jeremiah Washington had died in 1910 at the young age of forty-two. His wife Ruth had lived until 1931. Because the 1900 Census showed month and year of birth instead of simply a person's age, they were easier to find in the Maple Grove Cemetery. Ruth had a stone. While Jeremiah did not, he was listed on the cemetery index.

Holly had heard that Jeremiah's father lived from 1836 to 1892. The 1890 Census would have been immensely helpful, but all except a portion of the Wisconsin count had been destroyed in a massive warehouse fire. That state had purchased a portion of theirs already. Too bad Maryland didn't act fast enough.

The other snag was that there were a number of men named Washington who lived on the west side of Meadow Mountain during the same timeframe. Digger not only had to figure out who Holly's elusive great, great grandmother was (Jeremiah's father's wife), she also had to be sure who Jeremiah's father was.

Choices seemed to be among Charles, George, and Benjamin, with most online researchers believing that Jeremiah's father was Charles.

For the short term, Digger would go along with Charles, whose wife was named on the 1880 Census as Elizabeth. Charles and Elizabeth had a son name Jeremiah, but so did George and his wife Mary Elizabeth.

So many names came up in that time period. Charles and Elizabeth Washington lived only a few miles from where Holly grew up.

Digger put her head in her hands.

In family history research, an abundance of riches is not many names, it's the documents that prove those names are who you think they are. In Holly's family's case, that just might not be possible.

CHAPTER NINE

AFTER SHE SHOWERED AND dressed Tuesday morning, Digger went to the kitchen to look for Uncle Benjamin. Since Cherry had shown up, he spent less time sitting cross legged on the table. No sign of him.

She snapped a long lead on Bitsy and shoved him out the back door. "I know you want me to take you for a walk," he wagged his tail, "but I need to get to work. You can do your business and we'll walk tonight."

Tail down, he went down the back steps and immediately watered two bushes.

Digger raised her voice. "Where are you?"

No response.

She took an apple from the crisper and a granola bar from a cupboard and stuck them in her purse. Wherever he was, Uncle Benjamin didn't seem to want to talk. Very unlike him, but he'd never had a child around full-time. Did he get tired?

Digger quickly washed her dirty coffee cup and cereal bowl and placed them in the dish drainer. She called Uncle Benjamin one more time, and then went to the back door to let in Bitsy.

The dog made quick work of a treat. She added water and a few pieces of dry dog food to his bowls. He'd ignore the food until he was really hungry.

Finally, she couldn't delay longer. Digger took a lightweight jacket from the hall coat tree and reached for the front door handle.

From the top of the front staircase came Uncle Benjamin's voice. *"Digger. I heard you, but Cherry's resting. I didn't want to wake her."* He floated down the steps.

She took her hand off the doorknob. "Where do you guys hang out mostly? Your old bedroom?"

"Some there. She doesn't want to go outside, so we also go to Franklin's apartment. She likes to look out the window up there. You can see so far."

"I get why she wants to stay inside." When Uncle Benjamin shrugged his shoulders, she added, "She was outside, alone, for a long time."

"Of course. I'm hoping she'll want us to follow Bitsy outside one day. And come back in, of course."

"Did you have a chance to talk to her any more about what she remembers?"

He sat two steps up from the bottom landing. He almost looked tired. *"I've asked her questions a couple of time. She just mentions Samantha told her to hide in the hollow log and not come out until she returned. She insists they were playing hide and seek. Not sure she really believes it."*

"That doesn't make sense. If you both know where someone is hiding, the game doesn't work."

"From what I can gather, someone else was there. Or coming."

"But she doesn't know who that was?"

He shook his head. *"The two people she mentions are her mom and the man she calls the Yeller. Occasionally her grandfather."*

Digger thought for a moment. "It really sounds as if her mother was hiding her so someone else couldn't find her."

Uncle Benjamin nodded. *"I thought so, too."*

"And then what?"

"After that, she's very confused about time. To her, very little time passed. She looks the same, so she doesn't realize that she'd be, what, twenty if she lived."

"Did she stay in the log?"

"A lot, I guess. The raccoon was with her a good bit. She said it kept her warm."

"You don't get cold, do you?"

"No. I like to wear clothes that match the weather, but I don't need to."

Digger put her hand on the knob again. "She mentioned seeing light snow. Do you think she died in that hollow log?"

"Wondering about it. See if you can figure out the weather on the day they disappeared. I'd hate to think she died of exposure."

"I checked at work. Looks as if it got down to twenty-eight degrees. Unless she was warmly dressed...Anyway, it would be good to know whether she thinks the Yeller was her mom's boyfriend."

"I don't ask direct questions like that, but I'll keep listening to her."

TUESDAY MORNING WAS BUSIER than usual, but Digger and Holly welcomed it. A display ad they had done for the paper a few months ago featured many local small businesses, and it kept drawing attention to their work. Mostly companies wanted copies of pictures of their businesses, but at least it kept them aware of You Think, We Design.

Today, though, a local florist wanted them to design a display ad to use for the paper and in still ads on local cable. Digger spent much of the morning on that while Holly visited Duds and Suds to talk to Regina and Tyler about flyers to announce the grand reopening.

Digger planned to head to the library during lunch. She needed to find some of the local history books she'd promised to get for Uncle Benjamin, but she also wanted to look at high school yearbooks.

She kept thinking Samantha Halloway should have had more than two friends, should have had more written about her than an article every few years in the *Maple Grove News*.

Franklin barely remembered her, but he'd been ahead of her in high school. People usually remembered people in the grade or two ahead, not behind.

At least the name he remembered, Maybelle, was unusual. Maybe she had some ideas about Samantha's life at the time she disappeared. If they had kept in touch after high school.

At the library, Digger first checked the vertical files. The file cabinet with newspaper clippings of important events did indeed have a folder on the disappearance. The paper copy of the flyer was the same one she'd seen online, and other items interested her.

The Kids Who Move Dance Center had also done a flyer, which showed Cherry in a blue tu tu next to a ballet bar. Digger studied the happy face of a child who would be dead within a year or so. Her hair was piled on her head in a bun, and she clearly wore blush. She looked older than seven or eight.

A short letter to the editor, not in the paper's online index, was from "her best friend, Tina," and asked that the sheriff and "other polece" please find her friend, whom she missed very much.

"So, there really was a Tina," Digger muttered.

The other items were fairly short updates from the *Maple Grove News* through the years.

Digger closed the file drawer and pulled several high school yearbooks from the shelves and took them to a reading table. No one could accuse the Maple Grove High School of being crowded. Franklin graduated with seventy-two other fresh-faced eighteen-year-olds nineteen years ago. Twelve years later, Digger's class had sixty-eight.

She first found Samantha Halloway's picture. Her hair was shorter than she'd worn it later. If Digger had to describe her expression, it would be devil-may-care or mocking. Sort of affirming she would do what she pleased.

Digger studied each page, and finally came across Maybelle Grafton. Her perfectly straight hair seemed to be light brown, always hard to judge in a black-and-white photo. Though her narrow face appeared peaked, she had a flawless complexion and would have been pretty had she smiled.

Should she take the picture to the library staffer at the front desk? Why would she say she wanted to talk to Maybelle? Digger pondered that. Finally, she decided she could say she was doing advance work for a potential fortieth birthday party for Franklin and wanted to get a head start on finding his friends. Lame, but possible.

Digger approached the woman at the circulation desk, whom she knew only as Linda. Her eyes were glued to a book. When Digger stood in front of her, she looked up.

"Sorry! I didn't hear you walk up." She shut the book. "How can I help you?"

Digger relayed her ruse, and Linda studied the photo. "I don't know her, but I think she brought her little girl in here last Christmas, to show her the library. She said she spent a lot of time here. I'll be right back." She stood and walked into an office door not far away.

The bright posters on the walls mostly depicted pictures of books and animals. One with a dalmatian said, "I can spot a good book anywhere." A pink rabbit with huge ears advocated listening to books on your phone.

After several minutes, Linda returned carrying a three by five card. "Karl says since so many people know her, I can tell you her name is Maybelle Myers now, and she lives in Hagerstown. He doesn't know an address, but maybe the high school would have one."

Digger took the card. "Many thanks."

She almost forgot about Uncle Benjamin's books. It took several minutes to find two he might like, one on Maryland Civil War history and another on Garrett County's development in the 20th century. They should keep him busy.

She had just checked them out when Marty came into the library. The surprise she felt was mirrored on his face. "What are you up to, Hofstedder?"

He stood next to her. "Background research for a story. Catch you later." He headed for the circulation desk.

Digger watched his back for a second and then headed for her car. He'd blown her off, probably because she hadn't followed up on his "make up your mind" edict. Edict. That wasn't fair, she supposed. But nothing about her Uncle Benjamin/Marty conundrum felt fair.

Digger sat in her car and searched on her phone for Maybelle Myers' number. When she found it, she didn't bother to try the birthday party excuse. She introduced herself and said she was Franklin's cousin. That brought recognition, but Maybelle still sounded wary.

"I happened to walk past Samantha's old cottage, and it reminded me about her and her daughter."

Maybelle sighed. "The first few years after they disappeared, I had calls now and then. It was hard on me, but I guess people eventually forgot about them."

"I'm sorry to bring it up." Digger didn't really mean that. "I don't want to make you feel bad."

"We've all had to eventually recognize that they aren't coming back. Now that I have an eight-year-old myself, I find it even harder to think about."

Digger did some quick math. Based on when they graduated from high school, Samantha had had Cherry immediately after graduation. Perhaps she was even pregnant during school. In contrast, Maybelle had had her daughter in her early thirties. Or maybe the little girl wasn't her first child.

"When I had Bailey," Maybelle continued, "I thought that if she'd been...around, Cherry could have babysat for her."

"I'm sorry things didn't happen that way." When Maybelle said nothing, she added, "I do family history research as a hobby, and some of those skills would apply for finding people who've adopted new identities. I helped someone with that a few months ago."

"I saw the articles about you working with the Stevens family last year. Is this now a job for you?"

"No. I have a bad habit of getting an earworm about something and not being able to get rid of an idea. I wonder if you think it would be productive to look for Samantha and Cherry?"

"Gosh, I don't know. I always figured that her father must have paid people to look through the years." She hesitated. "Cherry was old enough that she would know where she lived back then. I wonder if she would have tried to return when she got on her own?"

"Do you mean if she were alive?"

Maybelle sighed. "I guess that's what I mean. It's been...a long time."

Digger had wanted to talk about Samantha and Cherry to see if her friends thought there was a chance they were alive. Didn't sound like it.

"You should really talk to Becky at the Maple Grove Grocery."

"Doesn't she do the flowers?"

"And produce," Maybelle said. "The flowers are busiest for Valentine's and Mother's Day. She says there's always carrots to sell."

Digger laughed. "Thanks. I hope I didn't upset you."

"No, Samantha was unique. Someday I'll tell my daughter about her."

Digger wished she'd said that earlier in the conversation, but now didn't seem the time to probe further. And she had to get back to work.

MARTY PERSUADED KARL Hindberg to talk to him by saying he was working on a story about how libraries served as resources for kids who did a lot of remote learning. He considered it a good enough idea that he asked Hindberg a number of questions and would actually do a piece on the subject.

Hindberg smiled as Marty closed his notebook. "I appreciate you reporting on this. Maybe you can do a sidebar that lists some of our resources.

"Sure. Send me a few and I'll add to it."

Hindberg began to stand, but Marty continued. "I've only lived here two years, so I've been going through a lot of old stories, familiarizing myself with the kind of topics people expect me to know about. You've lived here all your life, maybe you could help me with one."

Hindberg settled into his chair again. "Sure. What are you thinking of?"

"I'm doing a piece on the twelfth anniversary of the disappearance of Samantha and Cherry Halloway. I'm told you knew them well."

Hindberg's complexion went from sheet-rock white to tomato red in less than a second. "Where did you get that idea?"

Marty tried to look surprised, and then told a white lie. "My grandparents. Maria and Malcolm Wilson. They remembered that you were one of the people who put up signs, kind of scoured that area for them."

"Oh, right." His flush lessened. "I tried to encourage the sheriff of the time to do more. People seemed to think she just walked out of her life."

"But you didn't."

Hindberg shook his head. "The younger Samantha might have, but she was a good mom to Cherry."

"And you can't think of anything that would make her want to start a new life?"

Hindberg frowned. "Her mother died a year or so before that. They'd gotten close after she had Cherry. She missed her. But that didn't add up to running away."

Marty nodded. "I don't want to sound like a TV show, but can you think of anyone who would want to harm either of them?"

The flush returned. "That was barely discussed at the time. Why would you ask questions like that now?"

Marty smiled. "I guess it's all the years I lived in Baltimore. I didn't mean any offense." He stood.

Hindberg sat for a couple seconds more, eyes closed, then stood. "I'm sorry. I think of them often. Please don't sensationalize them."

"I won't. It just strikes me as a case people didn't think about long enough."

"I agree."

Marty sat in his car for almost a minute before he started the ignition. Karl Hindberg hadn't lost his temper in a traditional fashion, but he seemed like a guy who could have a short fuse. Maybe he'd helped look for the mother and daughter to be able to keep track of what the sheriff learned.

CHAPTER TEN

DIGGER SPENT TUESDAY AFTERNOON calling businesses in Oakland to introduce them to You Think, We Design. Most already had firms to help with form design or publicity. A fairly new business, which booked tourists for skiing in winter and Deep Creek Lake vacations in summer, needed business cards.

She thought they must come from a family of optimists, as the tourism business had barely begun to recover from pandemic restrictions. She took information on their website and said she'd familiarize herself with what they did and suggest some business card designs.

Holly had heard the conversation. "Hard to make a profit doing cards."

Digger grinned. "My devious idea is to suggest that we do the design and give them places they can order the cards online. That way we can send them a flat bill for graphics work."

"Very smooth," Holly said.

Her calls to Oakland reminded Digger she had wanted to talk to Maryann Montgomery, grandmother of Sheriff Roger Montgomery. The business card query from the (probably doomed) travel company had given her an idea.

"I'm going to call Maryann to see how she likes living in Maple Grove again."

"Tell her I said hello to that cute grandnephew of hers."

Digger grinned. "You're too old for him."

"Maybe he has an older brother."

Digger rolled her eyes at her partner and went to Maryann's name in her contacts list.

The lively ninety-year-old answered on the second ring. "Digger Browning. You need to come visit me."

Digger laughed. "I will. I figure you're unpacked and up to no good by now."

"It's hard to be up to no good here, compared to the senior complex in Oakwood. Not as many people and not as much to do."

"You sorry you moved up here?"

"No, I like being closer to family. I'm thinking of starting a weekly roulette game."

Digger mouthed "roulette wheel" to Holly. "Is that legal?"

Maryann laughed. "Not likely. But it would bring my grandson over here more often."

Digger realized she didn't want to talk about Hamil Halloway in front of Holly. "How about I stop by this weekend?"

"Weekdays I have fewer visitors."

"Do I have to call in advance or can I come if some weekday time opens up for me?"

"As long as it's not right after lunch, come anytime."

ON HER WAY HOME from work on Tuesday, Digger stopped at the grocery store. The produce department was near the entry, and the small area for displaying and arranging flowers sat between produce and the bread aisle. Digger supposed it had to be near a water supply, and there was plenty of water to spray on the vegetables.

Becky stood near the lettuce, checking items on a list. She and Digger knew each other enough to say hello, and she listened as Digger explained that a walk by the cottage had made her curious about Samantha and Cherry.

"I remember you helped find out what happened to that Mr. Stevens who vanished a long time ago." She shuddered. "Sam and I were supposed to meet the day they supposedly vanished."

Digger took note of the word supposedly, but didn't interrupt her.

"Cherry loved to go to the bakery and ice cream shop, where the Coffee Engine is now. So we were meeting there when I got off work."

"But they didn't show up?"

"No. In the before-Cherry days, Samantha would forget, or maybe ignore, a promise to meet people. But she really shaped up after Cherry was born."

"Did you try to call her?"

"Just once, while I was waiting. When she didn't answer, I left a message and figured she'd get back to me."

"But she didn't?"

Becky shook her head. "No. It annoyed me, but I didn't worry until her father contacted me late the next morning. Cherry often walked to the big house," she smiled, "that's what she called it, to have breakfast with him."

"By herself?"

"She was eight. Back then the state parks people hadn't widened that trail, so hardly anyone went up there. Samantha liked to sleep in. She'd get Cherry up and more or less dressed and go back to bed."

"But Cherry didn't show up for breakfast?"

Becky shook her head. "No, and that kind of started the ball rolling." She paused. "I imagine if Sam left for somewhere without telling anyone, you know, like left Cherry with her grandfather, that it wouldn't have caused much alarm. But Cherry loved school. Sam hadn't told her teacher Cherry would be absent."

"And she obviously hadn't told you or Maybelle she was heading out of town."

Becky nodded. "She didn't talk to Maybelle as much as me, since I live here. Sam was really a free spirit before Cherry was born. And after. But she loved her daughter and tried her best to be a good mom."

"This is a tough question..."

Becky smiled. "Do I know who Cherry's father is?" She shook her head. "I'm not even sure Sam did. She thought it might have been someone she hung around with in Ocean City a couple months before she knew she was pregnant."

"But she had no way to be in touch with him?"

"Them. She was often quite...active socially."

"Oh. And no boyfriend around?"

Becky shrugged. "People thought she and Karl Hindberg dated, but she always said they were just friends. I halfway thought he liked her more than she liked him, that she just wanted Cherry to spend some time around a decent man. You know, since there was no father in the picture."

Digger nodded. "I could see how a librarian could be a good role model."

"Oh, he didn't have that job back then. He worked in a couple restaurants and bars over in Deep Creek Lake, with the tourists."

Digger thought for a moment. "I don't recall anyone mentioning a job for Samantha, Sam."

"She occasionally worked here, before Thanksgiving and Christmas, when we hire temporary people. It was a bone of contention with her dad, but after her mom died, she didn't want to leave Cherry with anyone else."

"How did her mom die?"

Becky busied herself with restacking some oranges so they didn't fall onto the floor. "So sad. It was one of those mornings when things are just a little slick, but it hadn't snowed or anything. She slipped on the front steps, going out of the house."

"That's awful."

"What was worse was she might have been saved, but no one knew to look for her. She told Mr. H. that she was going to the beauty shop in town. He didn't realize she hadn't left until the shop called an hour and a half later."

"It was that cold?"

"I think it was more that the fall gave her what I think they called a brain bleed. By the time they got her to the hospital she was brain dead."

"Awful. So, how old was Cherry? You said her grandmother babysat for her?"

"Six or seven, and really close to her Nana, that's what she called her."

For the first time, Digger realized that Hamil Halloway had lost his entire family within a year or two. That could turn anyone into a recluse.

Digger thanked Becky and headed to the Ancestral Sanctuary. She shouldn't have left Bitsy alone so long. When she parked, she heard him barking nonstop. She ran up the porch steps and he nearly ran over her in his rush to get outside.

When he finished watering the grass he sat and stared at her. A reproachful look, if ever a dog could give one.

"I'm sorry, Boy."

"You should be."

She hadn't seen Uncle Benjamin and didn't like his tone. He stood just inside the door, with one arm around the invisible Cherry.

"You're right," Digger said.

"Cherry has been very concerned because Bitsy barked every minute or so for the last hour."

She looked to where Cherry seemed to be. "I'm sorry, Cherry." She couldn't say she had been trying to figure out how the child ended up in a log with a raccoon. "I'll make sure I leave work earlier tomorrow."

Uncle Benjamin stood back so Digger could enter the hallway. Not for the first time she wondered what would happen if she tried to walk through him.

"What if you put a doggie flap in the door that leads to the back porch?

They'd had this conversation previously. "Because to be big enough for a German Shepherd it would be big enough for a small child to crawl through."

"Cherry promises she won't go outside."

Digger smiled toward Uncle Benjamin's waist. "I know you wouldn't. But a small animal could come in, too, and..." She stopped.

Uncle Benjamin spoke rapidly. *"Not necessarily a raccoon, could be a fox. Even a bear cub."*

Digger made for the kitchen. He'd started this conversation. She'd leave him to handle it. She put her purse and the library books she gotten for Uncle Benjamin on the kitchen table and opened the fridge. Cheese and crackers would hold her for a few minutes.

Uncle Benjamin's placating tone came from the front hall. *"I know, sweet girl, but raccoons don't like car rides."*

AFTER DINNER, DIGGER KEPT her promise to take Bitsy for a walk. She tried to keep to the long driveway, but the German Shepherd picked up scents every few feet. Digger got pulled in every direction. "It's too bad Uncle Benjamin can't take you on walks."

After they had tromped by the large vegetable garden a second time, she was done. "Come on. I want to look at some more information for Holly." She tugged on the leash gently, in the direction of the house.

When they came in the back door, Digger could hear Uncle Benjamin's voice coming up from the basement.

"It's like I told you, Sweet Girl, you and I don't need to wash our clothes because we can just think about clean ones and we're wearing them."

Digger couldn't hear Cherry's response, but got the gist from Uncle Benjamin's reply.

"No," his voice drifted up, *"Ragdoll doesn't like the washing machine or baths."*

Digger hung Bitsy's leash on a hook near the back door and went to the large dining room table. She had carefully stacked what she thought of as the Holly Barton Files and began to spread them out again. She brought her laptop from the desk in the living room to the dining room and turned it on.

She pulled up the copy of Holly's family tree in her own account. Until now, she'd mostly tried to keep track of the varied Washington men – Charles, Benjamin and George – to determine which was Jeremiah's father. This time she focused on Jeremiah's wife, Ruth.

The 1910 Census had been done only two months after Jeremiah died and seven months after his and Ruth's son, Benjamin (Holly's grandfather), was born. Digger found a man named Samuel Martin in the same household as the widowed Ruth Washington. More important, she was head of the household, so his relationship to her was noted -- as her brother, older by three years. However, Martin wasn't necessarily Ruth's maiden name, if she'd been married before she met Jeremiah Washington.

Digger went back to 1880, when Ruth would have been two, and looked for Martin families in what had by then been designated Garrett County. She found Samuel Martin, Sr., and his wife Sarah. Their oldest son was Samuel, Jr. and they had two daughters – Ruth and Martha. Ages were a match. Success!

Digger went to the Find a Grave site and added Ruth's maiden name to her record and linked her to her parents. She loved being able to connect people and looked forward to telling Holly she'd found her Great Grandmother Ruth Washington's maiden name.

So, how did they help her find Jeremiah's father's wife's name? Now that she was connecting more of Holly's ancestors on Ancestry.com, the program had given Digger more hints.

Previously, she'd identified one Jeremiah Washington as a son of George and Mary Elizabeth Washington and another Jeremiah with Charles and Elizabeth Washington. Holly's Jeremiah had been born in 1868, but either one would have been the approximate age.

People didn't go as far from home in the late 1890s or early 1900s, which was when Jeremiah's parents would likely have married. Ancestry had two hints to Jeremiah's parents as Charles and Elizabeth, so Digger explored them and immediately saw why.

The property where Jeremiah settled with his wife Ruth was two households away from Charles and Elizabeth. In other words, very close to each other on the west side of Meadow Mountain. The son stayed close to his parents.

Digger felt more certain which family had Holly's great, great grandmother. "Bingo!" She didn't know Elizabeth Washington's maiden name, but she had a better starting point to find it.

Charles Washington (likely)

Jeremiah Washington

Elizabeth ?

Benjamin Washington

Samuel Martin, Sr.

Bessie Barton
Holly's Mother
Wife of Henry Barton
(born Washington)

Ruth Martin

Sarah (unknown)

Audrey Samuels

CHAPTER ELEVEN

WHILE HOLLY VISITED Duds and Suds on Wednesday, Digger held down the fort at the office, as Uncle Benjamin would say. She worked on designs for the business cards for the Oakland firm and then went online to find an obituary for Mrs. Halloway. Digger didn't know her first name, but soon learned that 'Nana' was known to those other than Cherry as Anita Halloway.

The obituary was brief, noting that she was a lifelong resident of Maple Grove who had "devoted her life to her family" and done volunteer work for the Maple Grove Hospice and the annual fundraising drive to ensure all kids had school supplies and winter coats.

She had also been a "quiet partner" in her husband's business, which the obit referred to as an investment advisory firm with clients throughout the country. Digger reread that sentence. She'd never given a thought to how Hamil Halloway earned a living. She assumed he was retired at this point, but he must have had a job to retire from.

The more useful article was the news piece that described how Anita Halloway died and the hand-wringing that had gone on afterwards. A local physician had discussed the need for prompt care after a head injury. The tone of the advice almost sounded as if he was quietly chastising Hamil or Samantha for not realizing she had fallen until it was too late to prevent her death.

Near the end, it described how her husband had driven her to the fire department in town so she could be transferred to an ambulance and taken to the hospital in Oakland. He hadn't wanted to wait for the ambulance to make its way to their home.

The article stressed the remote location of the Halloway property and mentioned that the family had owned property on the mountain since 1849. Hamil Halloway issued a brief statement to thank those who had assisted his wife, and Samantha was said to be too distraught to talk to anyone.

To herself, Digger said, "If she was distraught about her mother, imagine how she'd have felt if her daughter got killed."

WHEN HOLLY RETURNED FROM Duds and Suds, she brought a square cookie to which Regina had added frosting to make it look like a laundromat washer, complete with round glass in the door. "They said they enjoyed meeting 'you and your husband.' Is there something you aren't telling me?"

"Darn, I'd forgotten about that. Tyler said his wife wouldn't let him take pictures of the cottage because of poison ivy. We had no idea who they were, so Marty told Tyler his wife let him do it." She took a bite of the cookie. "I hope they didn't say it so other people picked up on it."

Holly grinned. "Just your old neighbor, Doug, what's his last name?"

Digger groaned. "O'Bannon. He never misses any reception or whatever. And he loves to jabber." She could picture the seventy-plus-year-old laughing at her from his front porch as she chased Bitsy down the street near her former bungalow.

"You better go down there and tell them you're single. When they said something to Marty, he got red and next thing I knew he took a couple pictures and left."

Digger grabbed her purse from under her desk. "I'll stop by the paper on the way. I'll make him squirm for a minute." In reality, she wanted a reason to see him and not feel like she was walking on eggshells.

She waved at the owner of the children's clothing store as she walked out of the building. She thought of walking the two blocks to the paper, but wanted to stop by the library afterwards.

The *Maple Grove News* had recently spruced up its front area with fresh paint and new tile, but it still looked like a classic, small-town paper. A large counter bore a stack of last Friday's edition with a coffee cup next to it so people could deposit a dollar if they took one.

No one sat at any of the three desks behind the counter, so Digger dinged the metal bell that sat next to the pile of papers. Marty's office was opposite the counter at the far end of the reception area, but she heard his voice from down the hall behind the counter, likely from the editor's office.

Marty called, "Be right there."

Digger didn't answer. Let him be surprised to see her. As he came into the reception area, she kept her face serious and pointed a finger at him.

"Aw, Jeez. I was going to call you."

Digger smiled. "Holly said Doug O'Bannon was offended he wasn't invited to the wedding."

From down the hall the editor called, "What wedding?"

Digger yelled back. "I thought you had an editorial to write."

Marty came to the counter. "That'll endear you to him." In a lower tone he added, "Sorry if I ruined your reputation."

"It's okay. Holly didn't seem to think you set them straight, so I'll head over there. When we ran into them it looked like you and Tyler had the same sense of humor."

"Yeah, are you...?"

From the hallway came an irritated voice, "Hofstedder, I got a couple more comments on this article."

He grinned as he turned away. "My piece on the Halloway update."

Digger found herself wishing he had asked if she was free for lunch. Then she decided she could have asked him, and chided herself for thinking like a teenager.

AFTER ASSURING TYLER AND Regina that she loved the laundromat's new look and telling them Marty was a comedian, she drove the four blocks to the library.

Digger couldn't barge into Karl Hindberg's office and say, "Tell me what you know about Samantha Halloway and her daughter's disappearance." A tactful approach would make him more likely to talk to her, and she also might need to deal with him later for historical society business.

Last year, Thelma Zorn had convinced Karl to devote a couple more shelves to local history. As a branch library, Maple Grove's was only about one thousand square feet. The historical society itself was much larger. However, materials in the library were more accessible to people, especially kids doing research projects. No way did Digger want to tick off Karl Hindberg.

Digger returned the book on Garrett County in the twentieth century that she had taken out for Uncle Benjamin. He had read it and pronounced it boring.

Linda was at the front desk wiping returned books with a sanitary cloth. "Hey, Digger. Did you get a lot of names for Franklin's party?"

It took several seconds to remember the story she had initially constructed to get Maybelle's current information. "Still working on it. That's the advantage of starting early."

"Good idea."

"So, Linda, I wondered if I could talk to Karl for five or ten minutes. It doesn't have to be now."

"He's working on the library's budget submission. I bet he won't mind a short break." She stood from her stool and went into the office behind the circulation desk.

Digger studied lists of bestselling books and community announcements on a bulletin board. Linda returned after a minute wearing a solemn expression. "He said he can give you two minutes."

Karl Hindberg's office was as compact as he was, giving the impression of efficiency to the point of severity. He did not rise from his desk as Digger entered, but kept reading some notes for another five seconds. Finally, he looked up. "Digger. I knew your uncle but don't believe we've formally met."

"We have not. Thanks for seeing me."

He pointed to a chair of light wood and a mauve cushion across from his desk. "I just have a short time. Budget season, you know."

She sat. "I do some current photography for the historical society, as a volunteer. We're trying to guess which activities or events will have historical significance fifty years from now or more. Digital photography and articles let us retain a lot more than when we had to keep banks of file cabinets of material."

He nodded, his impatience barely hidden.

"I got to thinking that concept could apply to more recent events and wondered if I could talk to you for a minute about the disappearances of Samantha and Cherry Halloway."

His face reddened. "Popular week for that topic. Why would you think I would know about that?"

She frowned slightly. Maybe when she saw Marty in the library the other day, he'd been here to talk to Hindberg about Samantha and Cherry. She wished he'd mentioned that. "I'm sorry. I thought you were friends. I had the sense Samantha didn't keep in close contact with a lot of people. Were you in the same high school class?"

He sat back in his chair. Digger had the impression he thought she was implying they dated, to use the euphemistic term for sleeping together, and he didn't like it.

"We were friends, but after high school. One of the times she worked in the flower section at the grocery store she kind of flirted with me." He smiled. "She wasn't really interested; I think that was just her natural behavior toward men. I asked her out, she blew me off and gave me a daisy, and we were buddies."

Digger smiled. "Sounds like a good way to make a new friend. I'm sorry you lost her."

He sobered. "Sometimes I felt as if I was the one who cared the most. I pestered the former sheriff, took a bunch of flyers to all the beach towns on the Eastern shore. I mean, it wasn't summer, but she liked to go there."

"Did she usually tell you, tell her friends, when she was leaving?"

"Of course. Especially after...her mother's death was hard on her. I don't think they were close before she had Cherry, but they really bonded over that child. Anita spent time with her every day."

Digger nodded slowly. "What I hear people say most often is that they thought something happened because she wouldn't have pulled Cherry from school."

He smiled briefly. "More like dance class. That little girl loved to strut." He stared at a place over Digger's right shoulder, and then back to her. "How is this of interest to the historical society?"

"After twelve years, well, that's a long time. They aren't likely to come back." She took a leap. "Some people say they never left, if you know what I mean."

He flushed again. "And you think I would know where they're buried, is that it?"

Digger's eyes widened. "Of course not. You, Becky, her friend Maybelle. You think about her. When I read the older articles, it seemed as if their disappearance was a...a flash in the pan. Why didn't people scour the mountain, the towns near here, for months?"

He sighed and shook his head slowly. "I never understood. I begged her father to let me go into her cottage to look for clues. He didn't just say no, it was hell no. He'd let the sheriff deputies in and that was that."

Karl stopped for several seconds. "On the surface that may sound like some murder mystery. He killed her and didn't want people to look hard."

"But you don't think that?"

He shrugged. "No one can know anything, but I do know he loved Cherry. Samantha liked to carry on, and in high school and right after, she drank a lot. She calmed down after Cherry, but she was still a party girl at heart."

"A party girl without a job," Digger said.

"True. Her mom left her a little life insurance. And a policy for Cherry's education. It went into some kind of trust that couldn't be used until Cherry was eighteen."

"That meant Samantha didn't have to save a lot, I suppose."

"Samantha was very up front about that. In fact," he paused. "I never gave it much thought, but she was angry that her parents wouldn't pay for her to go to a culinary school. They wanted college or nothing."

"So maybe she left so eventually Cherry could choose for herself?"

"After her mother died, I tried to talk her into finding a job and leaving that cottage. She didn't get along with her father. But she liked not having to earn a living." He shrugged. "We even fought about it a couple times."

"Seems as if it would be awfully boring living far away from town. Especially if she was a social person."

Hindberg nodded. "The only time she thought much about a job was if her father gave her advice – his word; hers was he bugged her – about Cherry."

"Not a lot of jobs here."

"No. For the first week I held out hope that maybe she'd found something and left to prove to her old man that she could be self-sufficient. Obviously, I don't think that now. And Cherry would have wanted to see her grandfather. They'd at least have come back to visit and get their stuff."

Back in her car, Digger thought about Hindberg's description of his friendship with Samantha. He sounded genuinely fond of her. But if he argued with Samantha, would Cherry think of him as a yeller?

DIGGER MADE A POINT of leaving the office by three-thirty. She wanted to stop at the historical society for a few minutes and still get home before four-thirty, so Bitsy didn't upset Cherry by barking. "I can't believe a ghost child is dictating my schedule."

At the society, Uncle Benjamin's longtime friend Thelma Zorn was at the desk. "It's been too long, Digger."

"It has. I might come by again in the next couple weeks. He kept wanting me to write about the Underground Railroad in this area. I need to find the time."

Thelma nodded. "From what I know, there were more people freed in this area than escaped, but I think there were houses that helped folks from other parts of Maryland or Virginia make their way to Pennsylvania."

"I hate to say it, but I was probably in high school before I realized the Emancipation Proclamation didn't apply to border states like Maryland."

"Yes, President Lincoln didn't want to encourage Maryland and Delaware and the couple others to leave the Union. But it was more an issue in Southern Maryland than here."

Digger nodded. "Tobacco farming down there. Do we have any, I don't know, diaries or oral histories from the period? I helped with the society's index, but I don't remember any."

"I don't think so, but you might look at the couple decades after the Civil War. People who helped slaves escape wouldn't have written about it during that time period."

"Good point." Digger went to the shelves that dealt with Civil War era history and found one general book on the Underground Railroad. She moved to the part of the shelves that had family and personal histories.

She knew Thelma wouldn't let those leave the society, so she quickly took photos of a tiny volume called "Our Stories of the Mountain." She selected it because the second page was a faded photo of a group of elderly Black men and women standing in front of a small, frame church.

The volume contained scans of handwritten essays, mini-memoirs really. The typed table of contents didn't have full author names. Instead they were titles such as "Samuel's Time in the Mines," "Bessie's The Night We Were Almost Cot," and Thomas's Blacksmith Days."

A glance at her phone told her she had to get moving. She checked out the Underground Railroad book and she hustled to the Jeep.

When she got to the Ancestral Sanctuary, Bitsy wanted a walk, but Digger fastened his lead to the back porch lead and let him wander for the thirty yards or so.

Uncle Benjamin came into the kitchen as she washed her hands. "You look tired. Do ghosts get tired?"

"I've never fully appreciated the effort Clara put into taking care of Franklin. She worked some at the store as he got older, but she had him by herself for a lot of long days." He floated onto the table.

Digger sat in one of the rickety chairs she planned to replace. "Where is Cherry?"

"Napping. Seems to sleep a lot for a kid her age, but what do I know?"

"Does she talk more about her mother?"

"Not much. Did say she read to her, so I found a couple of Franklin's picture books that Clara had saved. Showed her how to go in and look around."

"Books. I talked to the town librarian, Karl Hindberg, who was friends with Samantha. He seems calm now, but maybe he wasn't always so chill. Maybe see if Cherry can remember more about the Yeller."

"That could upset her. What good would that do?"

Digger raised her arms in a shrug. "I'd like to find out what happened to Samantha. If we could find a body, it might bring her and Cherry together."

"She talks about the raccoon more."

CHAPTER TWELVE

ON THURSDAY, DIGGER HEADED to the Maple Grove assisted living building. She'd never been in any of the compact apartments. Maryann Stevens had a separate bedroom rather than just an efficiency, so she'd brought furniture Digger recognized from visits in Oakland. The pale blue loveseat fit neatly into the far corner of the living room and the small dining table, complete with mugs for tea, looked as if it had been made for the space near the breakfast bar.

Maryann herself appeared more relaxed than Digger had ever seen her. Her honey-gold hair was a shade lighter, and she still wore expensive-looking gold jewelry.

Digger lifted her hand for a fist bump as she entered. "You look as if this place suits you."

Maryann gestured to the loveseat and the two chairs across from it. "It does. With my friend Nellie gone, I don't miss Oakland as much as I would have before. And I love being near my brother's family."

Maryann settled in one of the high-backed chairs and Digger on the loveseat. Maryann looked at Digger's left hand. "I keep wanting to see some kind of ring there."

"Maryann! We don't even really date." She paused. She'd almost said "yet."

"Well now, that's just silly. You and Marty clearly like each other a lot. I think you're the hold-up."

"When you're playing shuffleboard or whatever, do they have any discussions about tact?"

Maryann threw back her head and laughed. "The advantage of being over ninety is that you can say what you want." She grew somber. "But I've also learned to value family more than ever. You lost your uncle, you had to move to that huge house and be all by yourself. Is that how you want to spend your life?"

Digger leaned into the loveseat. She wasn't exactly alone. "You said you like visitors. Do you think they'll come back if you put them on the spot?"

"Don't change the subject. You don't have to answer me, but I hope you know the answer yourself."

Digger sighed. "My cousin, Franklin, finished building an apartment in the attic. He comes out from DC at least a couple times a month. We're close."

"You know what I mean."

On impulse, Digger asked, "Do you believe in ghosts?" She was pleased to see that Maryann appeared nonplussed.

"It is something I think about." She pointed to the kitchenette. "Why don't you make us some tea? The electric kettle will only take a few seconds to come to a boil."

Digger stood. "You're playing for time."

"You bet I am."

Digger let her think without interruption while she made the tea. She remembered the amount of sugar Maryann liked, half a teaspoon, and added cream to her own. She placed the two mugs on the coffee table in front of the loveseat.

When she sat, she met Maryann's eyes. "Finished thinking?"

"Mostly. When my husband first died -- Roger's grandfather, Richard -- I often thought he was in the room with me. It wasn't solely because I was used to having him around. I truly thought he was in his recliner next to mine." She paused. "Sometimes I'd talk to him."

"You must have missed him a lot."

"I did. And I could almost hear my mother saying, 'It's okay to talk to yourself as long as you don't expect an answer.'"

Digger smiled. "I'll remember that line." Of course, people who saw her seemingly arguing with herself as she drove through town probably thought she was nuts.

Maryann sighed. "After a while I sensed him less frequently, and after I sold our house, I never felt his presence again."

Digger mulled it over for several seconds. "But he never spoke to you, right?"

"Not directly." She hugged herself. "A few times I thought he moved things. Not furniture. Little things."

"Like what?"

Maryann chuckled. "The first Christmas, I looked all over the kitchen for the recipe for this hot dip I make -- it's really good. Couldn't find it. I went to the store for a few minutes, and when I came back, the recipe card was sticking out from under the toaster oven."

"And you were sure it didn't stick out before you left?"

"Positive. Same with a list I had of all the family birthdays. It used to always be paper-clipped to the wall calendar. Then," she shrugged, "not anywhere to be found."

"But later you found it," Digger said.

"Yes, on the floor below the wall calendar. I think it had fallen under the refrigerator." Maryann pointed a finger at Digger. "It even had a piece of a dust ball on it. That definitely meant it had been under the fridge."

"It would in my house, too," Digger murmured. "I heard, or read I mean, that recent ghosts can't move solid things."

"So, your Uncle Benjamin can float around but he can't whack you on the fanny?"

Digger flushed. "I didn't say I'd actually seen him."

"You didn't have to." In a kinder tone, Maryann said, "He could be truly present, or it could be your imagination. If it's the latter, maybe you need time to heal. Finding him was a horrible time for you."

Digger leaned her head into the back of the loveseat. "Yes, but...ohmygod." She stood. "I have to go home. I'll be back." She almost lunged at the door to the hallway. Once out of Maryann's apartment she half-jogged to the exit and then ran to her car.

The main reason for not revealing Uncle Benjamin's presence to Marty was that she didn't know what would happen to him if she told someone. In paranormal terms, she was his medium. Did she betray him by acknowledging him? Would he vanish?

She drove quickly toward Crooked Lane Road and started up the mountain toward the Ancestral Sanctuary. "Be there, be there," she whispered.

Once beyond the confines of town she picked up speed. Then she slowed to the speed limit. She didn't need to join Uncle Benjamin in the ghost community.

She passed the Gardiners' property and turned right into the Ancestral Sanctuary's long driveway. Relief gripped her. Uncle Benjamin sat on the front steps, pointing to Bitsy, who was cavorting in a flowerbed. As she drew closer, she spotted several trampled crocuses.

Uncle Benjamin stood as she parked. *"Thought you said you'd be late."* He turned his head. *"Don't go too close to the burn barrel, Cherry. There's poison ivy."*

Digger laughed. "Ghosts get poison ivy?"

"Don't plan to find out. You look funny."

She regarded his outfit, which brought to mind a scarecrow. "Have you looked in a mirror?"

Uncle Benjamin looked down. *"Oh, right. We were playing Wizard of Oz again."* He changed into his normal oxford shirt and red cardigan.

Uncle Benjamin pointed to the porch steps, and Digger sat next to him. "I visited Maryann Montgomery. You met her, well, sort of."

"I remember. Older than I am. Moved up here, didn't she?"

"She did." Digger took a breath. "I kind of...alluded to you."

Uncle Benjamin grinned. "*In my present form?*"

"Yes. I asked if she believed in ghosts, and she said she thought her late husband was there for a time. She couldn't see him, but he could move lightweight things."

"*Huh. Opposite of...Bitsy, come over here.*" Uncle Benjamin snapped his fingers. "*He's been in the poison ivy for sure. You'll have to wipe his fur.*"

Bitsy did not respond to Uncle Benjamin.

Digger snapped her fingers. "Swell."

Sensing the prospective attention, the German Shepherd raced toward Digger, tongue out. She took a tissue from her pocket and stroked his head with it.

"*Cherry is here,*" Uncle Benjamin looked in front of himself. "*Okay. We'll have to...wait a second.*" He turned to Digger. "*You want to play hide and see*k?"

She smiled in the direction Uncle Benjamin was looking. "I have to go back to town. I will later tonight." She stood.

"*Wait a sec,*" Uncle Benjamin continued to focus on Cherry's location, then looked at Digger. "*If you see her friends Tina and Jennie, tell them she wants school to start so she can play with them.*"

"If I see them, I will." Digger suddenly realized this was Cherry's first trip outside. As the little girl raced after Bitsy, Digger said, "Cherry's in the yard."

Uncle Benjamin followed the child with his eyes. "*Told you it would be the dog that got her out.*"

Digger had driven halfway back to town before she realized she had not been the one to let Bitsy outside.

BACK AT MARYANN'S, Digger sank into the loveseat. "I, uh, had to check on something. Sorry I rushed out."

"Was your uncle still there?"

Digger covered her face with her hands. "Yes. And, um, a ghost child. A little girl who vanished twelve years ago." She peered at Maryann through her fingers.

Maryann took this in and peered into her empty teacup. "I'll take some more, if you don't mind."

Glad to have something to do besides meet Maryann's gaze, Digger complied. She glanced over her shoulder to see Maryann sitting perfectly still, hands folded in her lap.

When she carried the tea to the table, Maryann smiled. "I'm intrigued."

"That's a great word. You don't have to call me bat-crap crazy or say you believe me."

She smiled, almost sadly. "Though minds do play tricks on us, you have a pretty solid one. Sit down and tell me what you see and what makes you so sure you're interacting with your uncle. And anyone else."

Digger took a deep breath and dumped her mind. She started with Uncle Benjamin's appearance shortly after his burial, his need to stay at the Ancestral Sanctuary or with Digger, and some of the times when he'd interrupted conversations between her and Marty.

She blushed, but didn't mention that Uncle Benjamin had stood between them when Marty stooped to kiss her last weekend.

Maryann nodded several times, which Digger took to be encouragement more than agreement. She started to say something, but Digger interrupted. "And when we go places together, he can wander around. I mean, he's not a voyeur, but when we were in Oakland after Nellie died, he went to her apartment and listened to the police conversations, then he came back and told me about them. It was exactly what the police told us later."

Maryann's face had become rigid. "He was in my apartment?"

"I told him about you. And he remembered Daniel pretty well, so he rode to Oakland with me one day to see you."

She still said nothing.

Digger felt bile in her throat. "He acts like a regular person. I mean, he doesn't follow people into the bathroom or anything like that."

Her face relaxed. "As long as he wasn't checking out my bank accounts or underwear drawer, I guess it's okay."

Digger closed her eyes. She opened them and felt tears, which she quickly wiped away. "Now you know why it'll be so hard to talk to Marty about this."

"Yes," Maryann said, dryly, "don't need a third person in the bedroom, do you?"

Digger winced. "We can...go to Marty's. But the point is, Uncle Benjamin would always be in my house with us."

Maryann took a final sip of tea and placed her empty mug on the coffee table. "Okay. I'm halfway there about your uncle. What is this about a ghost child?"

"It's even less believable." She leaned back in the loveseat. "You may not have heard of this boulder that sits a good way up Meadow Mountain."

"I have not."

"I have no idea how it ended up there. One story says that during the Civil War, people on that part of the mountain rigged up a pulley system to move it up there. Supposedly the locals could shoot from behind it if troops attacked."

"Which side were they afraid of?"

Digger shrugged. "With Maryland being a border state, there were strong feelings on both sides. But I kind of figure it was Confederate sympathizers afraid of Union troops. The Baltimore and Ohio Railroad took a lot of Union supplies through this area."

"And what does an old boulder have to do with a ghost child?"

"Oh, right." Digger smiled faintly, thinking of Uncle Benjamin running down the path with Cherry in his arms. "It's called Old Knob, and there's a good path leading up to it. I took Marty up there."

"Kind of like walking your dog, is it?"

"Funny." She flushed. "Marty's grandparents live here, but he didn't grow up in Maple Grove. Anyway, there's an abandoned cottage that sits not far from Old Knob."

"Every reporter's dream," Maryann said.

"He wanted to go back and take pictures." Digger finished describing the trek and Uncle Benjamin's find. "At first, I wondered if she was a figment of his imagination."

"How do you know she isn't? Do you see her?"

"No. But he relays some of what she says. And it isn't anything he could make up."

Maryann's eyebrows went up. "Like what?"

Digger shut her eyes for a moment. "Like two of her friends. I would never have thought to verify their names, but I went to the vertical file in the library looking for info about Samantha. The file had flyers and stuff, but also a letter to the editor from a child named Tina. Cherry told us about Tina. They went to dance lessons together."

"And your uncle wouldn't have been likely to come up with the name?"

"It's not likely he knew the dance studio or owner. He'd sold the hardware store by then and Aunt Clara had died. He kept to himself more as he got older."

Maryann regarded her empty mug.

Digger felt almost desperate to convince her. "It's more than that. He plays with her, the cat can either sense or see her. His cat. My dog can't."

Maryann raised her hands to her shoulder in a gesture of surrender. "I believe you. Does this mean pretty soon you'll be running the Home for Homeless Ghosts?"

Digger put her head in her hands. "If I do, I'll move." She raised her head. "I wanted you to help me with something."

Maryann smiled. "I don't know the Ghostbusters."

"I don't think I want that. Yet. Cherry's grandfather is still alive. Hamil Halloway. Do you know him?"

"I know the family name. When my parents ran the family dairy farm, they delivered fresh milk for a time. They didn't pasteurize it, and eventually people wanted only pasteurized milk. I used to ride with my father sometimes when he delivered it."

"And you went to his home? It's about halfway up the west side of Meadow Mountain."

"I don't recall him, but I remember the place, I think. Large frame house, with brick on the side that had the fireplaces. Unusual feature."

"That's it. You're ninety. I bet he's only in his late seventies, maybe a little younger."

"I don't remember children at that house, but my father never let me get out of the truck. My mother didn't like me going with him, but I would beg sometimes until they let me."

She stared past Digger for several seconds and then looked at her. "My brother Daniel helped him with deliveries as he got older, but when the war came, he was off. I guess that's about the time my dad stopped the deliveries."

"So, you never met Hamil Halloway?"

"Don't think so. What is it you want?"

"I want to know more about what was going on when his daughter and granddaughter disappeared."

She shrugged. "How would I even bring that up?"

"I think Marty's going to do a story about the cottage. People here may talk about it, and you can ask questions."

When Maryann said nothing, Digger added, "Now that we know Cherry died at about age eight, it's a good guess her mother died at the same time. If I could find her mother's grave, or learn how she died, maybe I could help Cherry."

"You want the mother's ghost to move in?"

"I'm kind of hoping that Cherry can join her. One less ghost to hang out at my place."

CHAPTER THIRTEEN

MARTY'S FRIDAY ARTICLE IN the *Maple Grove News* had an air of speculation his editor didn't usually permit in news stories.

The twelfth anniversary of the disappearance of Samantha and Cherry Halloway is in two weeks, and this weekend would be Cherry's twentieth birthday. While the image the public has is of an eight-year-old little girl, today she could be a mother herself.

The whereabouts of the two women remains a mystery, and those who were interviewed at the time had little to add.

Though new information has not been brought forward in years, the case remains open. Sheriff Roger Montgomery agreed with a statement that "someone must know something."

From behind Digger, Uncle Benjamin said, *"Bet a lot of people want to read that article. Always good to raise suspicion."*

"I don't think he'd say something that isn't true." She glanced at Uncle Benjamin and grinned. He wore a red hat with a wide brim and a red and white necklace. "I take it you're playing dress-up again."

He looked glum. *"And hide and seek."* He looked behind him. *"Gotta run."*

Digger shook her head and went back to the article.

Sheriff Montgomery had been with the Office of the County Sheriff for less than a year at the time of their disappearance, but he remembers it vividly. "A woman doesn't leave her family and friends without letting people know she plans to be away." At the insistence of Samantha's father, Hamil Halloway, he said they decided almost right away to assume she likely did not leave of her own accord. "And, of course, there was the little girl to think of."

When asked to describe the actions the sheriff deputies took, Montgomery said they notified, via fax and email, other departments in the state. They also created a flier to circulate, and -- with Mr. Halloway's permission -- searched the cottage on his property where Ms. Halloway and her daughter lived. "We found nothing to indicate foul play. Or any other reason they may have left."

From all accounts, including recent interviews, Samantha appeared cheerful, even happy, the day before. The now-retired tap dance instructor at the Kids

Who Move Center reported that Cherry had started to learn a new routine and seemed very excited about an upcoming recital.

Samantha was said to have dated a couple of men over the past year, but there had been no drama, as a girlfriend said at the time. The identity of Cherry Halloway's father had never been stated, so there is no option to ask if her father knows her whereabouts. Hamil Halloway again requested privacy.

The Maple Grove News received periodic reports of sightings for the first few years, all of which were explored and shared with law enforcement. None led to any concrete information about mother and daughter.

Today, the cottage the pair lived in remains boarded up on the east side of Meadow Mountain, a lonely reminder of lives that may have been cut short twelve years ago.

She finished the article and stared straight ahead. Marty talked to Cherry's former teacher and Sheriff Montgomery. Cherry didn't seem to expect to leave town permanently. Digger, of course, knew all the child had done was hide in a log.

Digger raised her eyes and stared at the window above the kitchen sink. If Samantha planned a disappearing act, she probably wouldn't have told Cherry. Samantha could have been cheerful because she knew they were about to start a new life. Neither of them would have behaved differently if they were about to be murdered.

The article, like those before it, did not name a boyfriend or Cherry's father. The lack of a regular boyfriend seemed unusual for someone Samantha's age, but not completely unlikely.

How would former boyfriends feel about having been referred to in a newspaper article? Specifically, would the reserved Karl Hindberg be sorry people might try to learn who Samantha dated?

Uncle Benjamin floated down the back staircase, minus his costume. *"Cherry hid in your closet, and she fell back asleep."*

"You want to finish reading the article on Samantha and Cherry?"

He floated over and studied it. *"Not a lot that's new, is there?"*

"True, but it's been a while since there's been an article this detailed. Maybe someone will think of something and call Marty."

"Wishful thinking."

"Does Cherry know tomorrow is her birthday?"

"I don't think so. Did you want to bake her a cake?"

Digger started to make a smart aleck comment, but realized he wasn't kidding. "I think that would be really confusing for her. And she might want to invite her friends to a party.'

"Good points. He looked at the article again. *No quotes from old man Halloway."*

Digger smiled to herself. "Isn't he a few years younger than you?"

"But he stayed home like an old person."

"Maybe if he won't talk to Marty, he'll talk to me."

Uncle Benjamin raised an eyebrow. *"He can be pretty grouchy. Why bother?"*

"I wouldn't care if we hadn't found Cherry."

"I met him at the bank one day. Not sure who does his shopping, but he never came to town. Invited him to a historical society meeting. Damned rude, he was. Said we just wanted to ask him for money."

Digger threw her arms up. "I need to do something. I keep thinking it could help Cherry if I visit him to learn more about what happened to her mother. Maybe he has ideas that didn't make it in the paper."

Uncle Benjamin's face had a panicked look and he glanced behind him. *"Cherry is at the bottom of the back stairs. She wants to know if she can come see Grandpa with you?"*

Digger winced.

"Cherry is joining us at the kitchen table," Uncle Benjamin said.

"Hi, pretty girl. You remember how we've explained that I can't see or hear you?"

Uncle Benjamin listened for a few seconds, then looked at Digger. *"Cherry asks if you can't see her, how do you know she's pretty?"* He stared toward where Cherry seemed to be. *"I told her about your pretty wavy hair."* To Digger he added, *"It's in a ponytail today."*

"Sounds lovely. I don't think your grandfather could see you either. It might be hard for you to see him and not be able to talk to him."

After a pause, Uncle Benjamin said, *"She wants to know what about Big Eyes? She misses him even more."*

"Of course," Digger said. "He's your friend."

Uncle Benjamin said, *"I think if you and I went there together, with Digger, that we might be able to find him. I can't promise he'd still be there."* He regarded the spot where Cherry seemed to be sitting, and then looked at Digger. *"Cherry feels certain Big Eyes would wait for her."*

Digger thought it interesting that Cherry missed the raccoon even more than her grandfather, but decided not to ask why. She might form her own opinion after she met the man. "Can we talk more about this tomorrow, Cherry?"

After a lengthy pause, Uncle Benjamin said, *"We're heading upstairs. Cherry wants to play with her doll."*

Digger didn't ask how an apparition played with a solid doll. She hated to disappoint even a ghost child, but she wasn't sure they should take her to the cottage right away. Before she could decide whether to talk to Uncle Benjamin about false promises, her cell phone rang. Marty.

She answered. "Long article, Hofstedder."

Silence.

"You there?"

He cleared his throat. "I've already had a call."

Digger looked toward the back stairs. "That's great."

"It would be, except it was from a very annoyed Hamil Halloway."

"Annoyed? He should be glad you made people think about it again."

"Puzzled me, too." Silence.

Whenever they came to the end of a phone call, Digger had the sense that Marty was waiting for her to tell him something. "I…"

But he had hung up.

Digger rested her elbows on the table and put her head in her hands. If she told Marty the truth about

Uncle Benjamin and now Cherry, would he think she was nuts? If he revealed something like that to her, she might think he was delusional.

And if she didn't tell him, she'd lose the friendship and the man she thought she might be falling in love with. But the only way to know that would be to spend time together. Without a ghost.

If she didn't have Cherry to worry about, she could ask Uncle Benjamin to stay in Franklin's apartment. No, that wasn't fair. Maybe she could put all of the family history files and books about local and state history in one place. And what? Lock him in there?

She stood and walked to the back door. From there she could see the small cemetery plot. Why hadn't Uncle Benjamin stayed there like everyone else? She flushed. She didn't really want him fully dead – not most days, anyway.

She took a sweater from a kitchen chair, unlocked the door, and almost ran down the back steps. She wouldn't find any answers with her ancestors, but maybe the questions would get clearer.

WHEN SHE RETURNED TO THE kitchen, Digger had made up her mind. She couldn't really start talking to Marty about Uncle Benjamin if Cherry were still in the picture. One apparition she was related to could be at least conceivable, but it would sound crazy to say she also lived with a ghost child Uncle Benjamin found in a log.

If she could figure out what happened to Cherry and her mother, maybe she could find where

Samantha's body was buried. She had to be dead. Otherwise, she would have come back for Cherry.

Unless she had deliberately left Cherry in that log. But why? Was she tired of being a single parent? Depressed about her mother's death? Tired of arguing with Hindberg about why she should get a job and get out on her own? Or maybe she wanted to be a free spirit again.

Maybe she got frustrated and Cherry's death was an accident. But Cherry seemed to imply her mother put her in the log to hide her, not hide her body.

If she could find Samantha's body, maybe she could find her ghost. If she found her ghost, maybe Cherry would want to be with her mother. Let them haunt Hamil Halloway's house.

Hamil Halloway. News articles mentioned few police conversations with him. He had always asked for privacy. She wasn't going to give it to him.

Digger opened a kitchen drawer and took out the very small Maple Grove phone book. She couldn't remember the last time she'd used it. She flipped to the H listings. Less than half a page, but there he was, "Halloway, H."

She pictured the house through the trees near the cottage. When it was built, access to what little there was in Maple Grove would have been hampered by snow, ice, and muddy roads. The Halloways had to bring some of their building materials in by railroad. If the rails could haul Union troops and supplies about fifteen years later, they had to have brought old-time stoves and other essentials that couldn't be easily made so far from a city with factories and stores.

Digger had no idea whether earlier generations of Halloways had been involved in various professions in town. Whatever they had done in the past, the seeming last member of the clan preferred to stay hidden away.

She lifted the receiver from the kitchen wall phone before she lost her nerve. After six rings, she pulled the phone away from her ear and was about to replace it when the ringing stopped.

It seemed someone had picked up the phone, but no one said anything.

"Mr. Halloway? Is this the Halloway residence?"

No hello, just, "Who's calling?"

"My name is Digger...Beth Browning. We haven't met, but..."

"I know who you are."

She took a breath. "I do a lot with the Maple Grove Historical Society, and I think you probably have a lot of memories tucked away in your brain. I would love to get to know you."

Tucked away in your brain? She felt like an idiot.

"I'm not interested in going to any meetings, Miss Browning."

"I don't like them either. I just...there are so many conversations I wish I'd had with my uncle, Benjamin Browning, before he died. I always thought he would be there. You probably know a lot about Maple Grove from its early days."

He actually chuckled. "I'm not *that* old."

She almost stuttered. "I know, but a lot of families talk about how their parents and grandparents lived, what they did. I think your house is the last of the larger ones on your side of the mountain." Digger waited for a response.

"I suppose you could stop by. Alone. And if you plan to talk to me because of the article in the paper, be assured I don't discuss my daughter and granddaughter."

"Of course not. The article did prompt my interest in you and your family, but the only publication I write for is the historical society newsletter. I do have an idea…well a thought about how to see if they're still alive."

He said nothing for so long that Digger was about to ask if he was still on the phone.

"Okay, Miss Browning. I'll be here all day. Why don't you come up about three PM?

MARTY STARED OUT OF HIS office window to the paper's worn parking lot. He chided himself for calling Digger. He may have first seen the cottage when hiking with her, but he certainly didn't need to know her reaction to the article. "Stupid."

From the doorway, a man's voice said, "If you're talking about Roger Montgomery being ticked off about the piece about the Halloways, I'd agree with you."

Marty turned to face his editor, Wendell Hines. "Wonder why he didn't call me if he's ticked?"

Hines shrugged. "Guess he's had some calls. No, not tips, just questions. I think I'm supposed to rein you in."

"That was hardly investigative reporting."

Hines grunted. "For Maple Grove it reads like it. Montgomery never struck me as somebody who'd cover up anything."

Marty glanced at his computer screen, which he had open to his email. Several new items had popped up. "He's always struck me as a more or less straight shooter. Probably doesn't like getting calls when he can't tell them anything."

Hines turned. "Nothin'll come of it, but keep it up."

Marty read his emails. Becky James from the grocery store – he'd never known her last name – thanked him for the update. She wished she could do "something to bring some closure for Mr. Halloway."

Like everyone else he'd talked to, she assumed Samantha and her daughter were dead but went for the euphemisms.

Tyler's note said he hadn't realized Marty was covering a serious subject when they'd met near The Knob. He'd only moved to the area five years ago, and had no idea about the "very sad story."

The third email stopped him. "Leave. It. Alone." The sender had the kind of garbage email account that spammers used – lots of letters and numbers, sent from a Gmail address.

He stared at it for several more seconds. "Somebody wants to stir the pot." He saved the email to his hard drive, then hit reply. "Give me a call." He included his mobile number.

By the time he'd reached for his coffee cup, his email had bounced back.

CHAPTER
FOURTEEN

IF SHE HADN'T KNOWN the house was down the narrow, tree-lined lane, Digger would have thought the unpaved track was an access road for park employees. Instead, in about an eighth of a mile, the two-story, white frame house stood sentry. That perception was reinforced by a cupola that sat atop the second story, in the middle of the house.

Digger could tell it had been added after the initial construction, not because it looked new but because its appearance was incongruous with the rest of the structure. The lumber on the first two stories was narrow, while that on the cupola was almost twice as wide. Its windows were very different from the wood-hung windows elsewhere.

Like a lot of houses built in the nineteenth century, its foundation contained large piles of flat stone and brick. They were a good two feet above the ground, and she assumed the house had a cellar of either brick or limestone.

The Halloway house, however, had packed dirt next to much of the foundation, creating a berm of sorts. Perhaps that was a way to keep water out of the cellar.

As Maryann Montgomery had remembered, one side of the house sported aging brick, with two fireplaces on the first floor and one on the second. An odd configuration, but it had been built long before central heating systems.

The house had not been painted in years, but the modern green shutters appeared to be aluminum and the lawn looked well cared for. As she walked up the front porch steps, Digger noted how clean everything appeared to be. Not even a few dried leaves on the steps.

She used the large brass knocker and noted a curtain to the right of the door move. Soon the handle turned, and she faced Hamil Halloway. In a collared white shirt and black slacks, he seemed thinner than in the photo of the cottage, when he'd sported a red sweater.

"Good afternoon, sir. I'm Beth Browning."

He eyed her without moving. "I met your great uncle. I believe you're referred to as Digger."

She smiled. "A name I earned while visiting a cemetery with him when I was little."

He smiled briefly. "Please come in." He stood to one side so she could pass him.

The dark interior spoke of a lonely place. From behind her, he said, "The drawing room is to your right. I took the liberty of making coffee."

Digger was struck by his apparent cordiality, not what Uncle Benjamin had experienced. "Thanks so much."

She entered the room, which was at least sixty feet in length. Chairs and sofas were arrayed in three groupings. Hardwood floors gleamed. She looked at Halloway before sitting on a loveseat near a coffee table that held a thermos and mugs. "This is beautiful."

"Thank you. It looks the same as it did when my wife died thirteen years ago." He sat in a matching loveseat across from her. "For that matter, much of the furniture is from my grandparents' time, at the end of the nineteenth century. Anything made of wood. My wife selected these small sofas."

Digger nodded. "Thank you for seeing me." He gestured to the coffee thermos and Digger began to pour herself a cup.

"I don't usually have visitors, but as you can imagine, your comment about Samantha and Cherry intrigued me more than the history discussion."

Digger added cream and cradled the mug as she eased into the cushions. "I can't claim the idea. A young man I know wanted to learn more about a grandfather who vanished long ago, and asked me to teach him how to use family history websites to see if he had appeared elsewhere after leaving Maple Grove. In this case, I'd obviously be using more modern electronic tools than were available when people searched twelve years ago."

"In case my daughter reappeared, as you say, somewhere else?"

Digger nodded. "And perhaps your granddaughter, though she would be harder to find."

He spoke sharply. "And why would that be?"

"For one thing, she will look very different as an adult than as a child, and for another, she wouldn't have been issued any formal ID at age eight. There wouldn't be much to use for comparison."

He poured his own coffee and added cream and two lumps of sugar.

Digger couldn't remember the last time she'd seen anyone use lumps.

"And exactly what would you propose doing, Ms. Browning?"

She took a breath. "It would take time. I won't finish in a week. Many states have marriage records online..."

"She wouldn't have used her own name."

"Probably not, but she might have used a variation. She might want, for example, a similar first or last name. That way, if she starts to sign her name and uses the original one, it's easy to change course."

He shrugged. "What if she never changed her name?"

"My guess is your offer of a reward would have encouraged people to spot her. I'll look for similar names in online city directories, especially in towns in or near the mid-Atlantic beaches. I heard she liked to go to Ocean City, Maryland. She might have gone to a place she was familiar with."

Halloway stared above Digger's head. "And your interest arose simply from that news article?"

"Actually, I hiked up here last Saturday with a friend. We came back Sunday so he could photograph the cottage. I can't fathom losing someone so suddenly, with no information on what happened to them."

"You were with him that day."

She thought the statement was really a question. "Marty and I have been friends for a year or so. He didn't grow up in this area." Why she added that she had no idea.

His smile appeared more genuine. "You sidestepped that well."

Digger could feel her face reddening. "Friends, really."

He sighed and put his mug on the coffee table. "This will probably sound terrible to you, but my daughter and I butted heads a lot. I'm sorry she ran away, if that's indeed what she did. But it's my granddaughter I really want to find."

Digger nodded slowly. "She also didn't have a lot of choice in the matter, since she was eight."

He nodded. "I don't mind if you look. What is your fee?"

"Fee? No, I meant, I'll look. Like after work and weekends."

His eyebrows went up. "You have many unused hours in your weeks?"

Digger laughed. "I should be drumming up more work for our graphic design business and painting the inside of my old house." She sobered. "This could be more rewarding. If I find information."

"Certainly for me. You want nothing in return?"

"No, I..." She glanced around the room. "Uncle Benjamin shared his love of history and anything old. If you ever want to give me a tour of your house, or at least part of it, I'd love to see it."

He placed his mug on the table. "It's interesting what people value. This place is old hat to me." He stood. "Come on, I'll show you the first floor."

Digger was no stranger to large, older homes, but she'd never been in one quite as elegant as the Halloway house – at least not one that was built so long ago. Its paint-worn exterior had led her to expect an interior reflecting the house's age. To an extent it did. Older wallpaper had classic patterns in beige and brown with dark blue flowers thrown in. It looked very expensive and showed no wear.

He led the way. "Let's start in the kitchen. My mother always said it was the hub of any house."

They walked across immaculate hardwood floors, and Digger wondered who kept them in that condition. Surely Halloway didn't use floor polish himself. The dining room held one large table, likely maple, with six high-backed chairs. The room was so huge another dining set would have fit comfortably.

When they got to the kitchen, Digger gaped. She had not expected a refrigerator with an icemaker, stainless-steel dishwasher, or granite-topped counters.

He took in her amazement and smiled. "Thought you'd see butcher-block counters and an icebox, did you?"

She took in the deep green walls and oak chair rail. "Kind of. But how...when did you do all this?"

"Over the last five years. I purchase from a home design place in Pittsburgh and use their installers. That way there isn't a lot of local talk about how I spend my money."

"If I ever get a lot of it, I'll have to remember that." Though she wouldn't. She'd go to Uncle Benjamin's former hardware store.

At the back of the kitchen were three doors. She assumed one went to the basement and another led outside. The third intrigued her. "You have a butler's pantry?"

"In a house like this, yes, of course." He gestured that Digger could head that way.

The door sat across from the one that led onto a large back porch. As with similar spaces, the butler's pantry walls were lined with cupboards and each side had a counter.

The counter on the left was wider with equally wide cupboards beneath it. The one on the right had shelves of staples and paper goods, and a narrower counter space. Between the top cupboards and the counter was blue wallpaper.

A door across from the pantry entry likely housed a smaller closet with fine china and silver. On the right side was a narrow door that would have to lead to the dining room.

Halloway took notice of her scan. "You didn't see the door in the dining room because it's covered with the same wallpaper as the room, and that side has no handle. It only opened if a butler of old served food."

"Very elegant." Among her churning thoughts was that if the house had been a stop on the Underground Railroad, it could have many hiding places.

She backed out of the pantry and nodded toward the wide door that likely went to a cellar. "You must have a huge cellar. I've heard talk that this house was used for the Underground Railroad."

"If you listen to local wags, some people think that. I asked my parents several times, and each time they said no."

"That's too bad. It means there isn't any house left on Meadow Mountain, that I know of, that served as a station."

Halloway leaned against a granite counter. "Most houses of that period are long gone. I had always heard that the family closest to this property, the Hurders, helped a number of people. I don't know that it was true."

"So, no one up here was a slave owner?"

"I didn't say that. My family was not. The Hurders had a blacksmith shop on the property and a small one in town, in the area that's now the town square. I'm told they had a few men who worked on that, all members of one family."

Digger frowned. "Odd that they would help slaves escape if they had some."

"What I've heard is that the Hurders promised the men freedom but asked them to stay as sort of a cover for their work to help others escape."

"That sounds like a romanticized version of bondage." She would have to check census information for the Hurder family. If the slaves were all men, that would not shed light on Holly's great, great grandmother.

Halloway turned toward the front of the house. "I suppose so. During the Civil War, this was hardly a well-populated mountain. It wouldn't have been impossible to sneak down the mountain and hop on one of the boxcars with supplies for the Union Army."

AS SHE DROVE HOME, Digger reflected on her conversation with Hamil Halloway. He'd been polite, cordial even. But she didn't see any signs of pain or loss when he talked about his daughter and granddaughter. It had been a long time, of course.

She didn't know what she had expected to learn by visiting him. Yes, she did. Something about Cherry. If she died in that log, someone must have removed her body.

Halloway had been twelve years younger then. Had he roamed the property looking for them? But why not say if he found the little girl's body?

Her cell phone buzzed as she turned into the Ancestral Sanctuary's long drive. She glanced at it. Maryann Montgomery. She stopped the car and answered. "How's my favorite senior citizen?"

"I bet you say that to all the girls."

Digger laughed. "What's up?"

"I've been listening. There was a lot of talk today about Marty's article about the Halloway disappearances."

Digger put her Jeep in park. "What kind of talk?"

One of the men at my lunch table had a daughter in the same high school class. I didn't get her name, his is Cornell."

"First or last?"

"First. I should know his last name, but I don't. Anyway, he said that this Samantha had never gotten along with her parents, especially her father. After her mother died, Samantha thought about leaving the area. I guess she got some insurance. She wanted away from her old man, that was the phrase Cornell used."

"Her mother had been dead for more than a year. I wonder why she didn't go?"

"Cornell said it could have been gossip, but that her father wanted that little girl to stay. He said he'd get the court to assign him guardianship."

"Good Lord. I haven't heard anything like that before."

"And it doesn't really make any difference at this point, does it?"

Digger thought for a moment. "It could have given Samantha a strong reason to leave and her father a stronger reason to try to force her to stay."

"True, but surely someone would have heard from her if she were still alive."

"I think so, too. She would have eventually run out of any insurance money."

"And as a mother, she would have wanted her daughter's killer brought to justice," Mary Ann said.

Unless she did it, Digger thought.

CHAPTER FIFTEEN

THE ANCESTRAL SANCTUARY WAS oddly quiet when Digger unlocked the front door. Not even Bitsy came to greet her. She flipped on the front hallway light, walked past the living room, and looked through the dining room to the door at the back of the kitchen.

Bitsy and Ragdoll sat facing the back door, which told Digger that Uncle Benjamin and Cherry were probably outside. But Bitsy wouldn't know that. Or had he come to sense Uncle Benjamin? No, more likely he was simply there because Ragdoll was.

"You two don't come to greet the person who feeds you?"

Bitsy yipped and padded toward her and Ragdoll stood on her hind legs, paws on the door to the back porch.

"Okay, you can go out." She opened the door and they both raced into the yard. She followed more slowly and surveyed the area, finally locating Uncle Benjamin and Cherry in the family plot. Ghosts in a graveyard?

She shook her head and was about to go inside when she remembered coming home a few days ago to find Bitsy in the yard. How had he gotten out? Surely Uncle Benjamin would have mentioned if he or Cherry could open a door.

Puzzled, Digger put a pot on the stove to boil water for spaghetti and pulled a plastic bowl of frozen sauce from the freezer. Maryann's information bothered her. She'd never thought Samantha left in anger and stayed hidden, certainly not with her daughter dead. Could she have killed her? Would that be why Cherry's memories were so foggy?

She glanced at the kitchen clock. Marty would probably be home by now. She called from the house phone.

"I know this isn't Benjamin Browning, so hello, Digger."

She almost dropped the phone. "I forgot the phone was still in his name. You get a lot of reaction to your article?"

"Not really. After this amount of time, it isn't something I'd expect people to pay much attention to."

"I talked to Maryann this afternoon. She said it was a topic of conversation at her dinner table at the senior apartments."

Marty yawned. "Anything earth shattering?"

"A man whose daughter went to high school with Samantha said she was thinking about leaving the area, but her father threatened to try to get guardianship of Cherry."

"Huh. Who said that?"

"Maryann said his first name is Cornell, but she forgets his last."

"Not a common name. Just a minute."

Digger heard his fingers clicking on a keyboard, then he opened and closed a drawer.

When he got back on, Marty sounded more interested. "I searched an online database we subscribe to. No one with a last name of Cornell in Maple Grove, but there's a Cornell Grafton. Ring any bells?"

"Samantha's friend Maybelle's name was Grafton. Does he live at the senior apartments?"

"Just a phone number for him, so maybe. How did you know her friend's name?"

"Franklin didn't know Samantha. She was younger. He remembered just the name Maybelle as a girl Samantha might have hung around with. Only one Maybelle was in the high school yearbook the same year as Samantha."

Marty was silent for several seconds. "Did you talk to this Maybelle Grafton?"

"She's Maybelle Myers now, and she lives in Hagerstown. I called her."

"Why? Digger, are you getting kind of obsessed with this?"

And there it was again. Because Marty didn't know about Uncle Benjamin finding Cherry, she couldn't be honest about why she wanted to find out what happened to Samantha Halloway. "Like I told you at dinner the other day, it bugs me that she was here one day and then vanished. It shouldn't be that way."

"It's unnerving, I'll give you that. But it was a long time ago. What are you trying to find?"

Her turn to be silent for a moment. "I'm not sure. I'm looking at marriage records in other states, things like that. It's not likely she did a DNA analysis, and, anyway, I wouldn't have any way to compare it to her father."

"I guess people find long-lost relatives that way. Good luck. Probably see you next week around town." He hung up.

His clipped goodbye irritated Digger, but she understood his annoyance with her. She felt no less frustrated by trying to appreciate Marty's perspective.

Bitsy's barks interrupted her thoughts, and she went to the back porch. He sat by the bottom step, half covered in pine needles and dirt, tongue hanging out, seeming proud of himself about something.

"Stay." Digger grabbed a kitchen towel from where it hung on the oven door and returned to the dog. "Sit still while I brush you off."

He yipped and tried to lick her arm. When she finished, he took off toward the burn barrel.

"Come back here! I'm not cleaning you again." She glanced around the yard. Uncle Benjamin and Ragdoll stood next to the burn barrel, so that probably explained Bitsy's antics.

As she started toward them, Digger realized Uncle Benjamin was peering into the barrel. She knew she hadn't burned anything but brush, so couldn't imagine his interest. Then she drew closer and could hear him.

"I know you don't feel dirty, Cherry, but it's not a good place for hide and seek. Look at all the ashes in the bottom." He suddenly looked up. *"Come back down now."*

Digger stopped. She'd never seen Uncle Benjamin do more than float just off the ground. "Is she above you?"

He glanced in her direction and then back up. *"She's learned she can go high. I've never tried it."*

For a second, Digger thought she heard a child laughing, but the sound ended as quickly as it had begun. "I'm going to take Bitsy inside. I'm glad you guys can't track in dirt.

AFTER CHERRY WENT UPSTAIRS to read to Ragdoll in her bed, Digger found Uncle Benjamin diving into her pile of research materials on the dining room table.

He poked his head out of a stack of manila folders. *"Did you trace back Holly's ancestors by where they lived on the mountain?"*

"Some, but I have more to do. I have a question for you." She gestured. "Come on out of there, would you?"

He rose from the stack and sat on a blade of the ceiling fan. *"I honestly don't know why she likes to be high up."*

She patted the table. "The other day when I came home for a few minutes, you were outside with Cherry and Bitsy. How did my dog get out?"

Uncle Benjamin sat cross-legged on the table. *"Cherry said you left the back door open and Bitsy pushed on the screen. I meant to tell you to check the next morning, but I forgot."*

"I didn't leave it open. That means Cherry opened the door."

"That little vixen."

"Do ghost kids act guilty when they tell a lie?"

"Don't know. Can't be something she can do regularly. Just today she kept wanting me to open the refrigerator to see if we had ice cream. She forgets she doesn't eat. I reminded her she could go in and look around."

"So how did Bitsy get back in?"

"The door was ajar. Bitsy nosed it open."

"You'll have to keep an eye on her. What if she knocked over a candle?"

Uncle Benjamin sighed, and seemed dejected. *"I'll talk to her more. This is all new to her. Not sure she's even aware she opened the back porch door."*

"Come on, we'll go over some of Holly's ancestor stuff. That'll perk you up."

She opened the thickest folder and pulled out the handwritten pedigree chart she had fashioned for Holly. "Okay, we have: Holly Barton, not married. Henry Barton, her father, who married Bessie Washington."

"And it's the Washington side that has the questions."

"Yes. I've looked at some of her Barton background, but she wants to know her mother Bessie's side."

Digger continued. "Bessie Washington was the daughter of Benjamin Washington and your good friend Audrey, maiden name Samuels."

"I pity the Samuels," Uncle Benjamin said.

"Be polite. Benjamin's father was Jeremiah Washington, and his wife was Ruth, maiden name Martin."

"Last time we talked, you sounded as if you were more certain that Jeremiah's father was Charles Washington, but you had no idea who his wife was."

"Yes, and he appeared to have lived from 1838 to 1892, dying at fifty-four. Seems young to us."

"So now what?"

"I pulled up the will index last time I looked on the computer and found Charles Washington. But the online probate info only names survivors, not the whole will. His wife was Elizabeth and his children, Jeremiah, Rebecca, and Abraham."

"All Biblical names."

"One census record says he was a preacher. I haven't determined yet if he had a church. But Elizabeth is such a common name of the time."

"And not many marriage records for slaves, unless they were compiled later."

"Right. You told me a lot of freed slaves took the last names of their former owners."

He nodded. *"The historical society has some records of owners who freed their slaves."*

Digger nodded. "Among the families I found records of were the Hurders, who lived next door to the Halloways. But I haven't really dug into that yet."

"No time like the present."

Digger went to Ancestry and pulled up the 1850 and 1860 Census records for Halloway and Hurder families, which were on the same page, in adjoining households. "In both years, the Hurders are blacksmiths. In 1850, they have two adult male slaves in their 30s, a female between 25-30, a girl between 5 and 10, and a boy the same age."

"There were two blacksmith shops on the old square, before that 1902 fire took out the north side of it. You can look to see who owned them."

"I'll do that." Digger felt her excitement rise as she kept reading. "In 1860, the girl child is fifteen, listed with the family as a free person, mixed race."

Uncle Benjamin nodded and peered at the computer over Digger's shoulder. *"So maybe that little girl on the 1850 Census was the child of one of the Hurder men. They freed her before 1860."*

"And if she's the same child," Digger pointed at the screen, "her name is Elizabeth Hurder."

Uncle Benjamin whistled lightly.

Digger turned her head. *"I didn't know you could do that."*

"Cherry taught me."

"Great, now it's a school for ghosts. What do you think?"

"About the whistling?"

"No! The child."

"I'm just messing with you. I think it's definitely worth exploring. But…"

Digger sighed. "How will Holly take it if it's true and she isn't all Black?"

Uncle Benjamin resumed sitting on the table. *"Forty or fifty years ago, less in some places, I think it would matter more. Why don't you tell her you could be cousins?"*

"I'm not sure humor will be the best option when she first finds out." She yawned. "I need to look for the Hurder family in later censuses. The house isn't there anymore, you know."

"Don't think there's been a house on that land for more than a century. You can go to the old plat books and see what you can find."

Digger examined a page of the 1850 Census. "This is the first time the Halloway family appears in an Allegany County Census. H. and M. Halloway, no first names. Two kids, Hamil and Alexandra."

"So, the name Hamil has been used in prior generations. If you ever go back farther, I bet Hamil was somebody's maiden name a generation or so back.'

"Could be. Back then a lot of people married their next-door neighbors. I'll look for a link, but I don't really expect it."

Uncle Benjamin stretched. "Couldn't exactly hang out at the mall to meet people."

"Nobody does that anymore."

"Just trying to help."

Digger raised her eyes to the second floor and back to Uncle Benjamin. "I think I'm going to check for Cherry's raccoon tomorrow. If I find him, you want us to take her up there?"

"Sure." He had a hopeful expression and lowered his voice. "And let's look for her mom, too."

CHAPTER SIXTEEN

CHERRY HAD MENTIONED THE log several times, but since Digger and Marty had left the area soon after Uncle Benjamin found Cherry, Digger had never investigated it. If ghosts were going to be her primary companions, she wanted to understand their world better. And she was genuinely curious to see if the damn raccoon was still there.

She'd dressed for the gloomy Saturday in brown jeans and a dark green turtleneck. She would hardly be camouflaged, but she wanted to attract the least attention possible as she prowled the area near Samantha and Cherry's former home.

Digger took a fanny pack from her bedroom closet. When she got to the kitchen, she added a couple granola bars and a small bottle of water.

"Going on a trip?"

"More like a hike." She lowered her voice. "I want to see if Cherry's raccoon is still up there. If it is, we can let her see it. If the grouchy thing's gone, that's another reason not to take her up to the cottage."

Uncle Benjamin looked at the floor and back to Digger. *"I don't like you going up there by yourself. Wish I could be there. And not just because I'm bored silly."*

Digger leaned against the kitchen table. "Having Cherry here keeps you tied down."

He nodded. *"Can't leave her alone. Or I don't think I should."*

"We'll have to plan some...I don't know, visits to parks? The library children's section?"

"I'll have to explain that she can't expect to talk to you in a place with other people."

"Hey, what if I left the TV on when I go?"

"But it's only for watching DVDs. We don't get channels."

"I bought a digital tuner and a small antenna." She stood and walked to the living room. "See that black patch on the side window? It usually only gets PBS, but Cherry could watch it, and so could you."

"You'd have to leave it on. Don't want her frustrated if she can't pick up a remote."

Digger flipped on the TV and kept the volume low. "She still doesn't understand she's a ghost?"

"Sometimes she does. You should have seen her the day she floated through the door to her room."

"She liked it?"

"Not at first, but she got used to it." He shrugged. *"But then she talked about sneaking up on her friend Tina, so it's complicated."*

Digger pushed herself away from the table. "I guess what I'm hoping is if she was up there all this time that her mother is nearby. I don't want a houseful of ghosts, but if we had Samantha, Cherry could stay here with her while you and I go gallivanting."

Uncle Benjamin smiled. *"Or at least over to the library in Frostburg so I could dive into some history books I haven't read."*

BY THE TIME SHE began the trek up the trail, Digger had begun to laugh at herself. She was hiking toward an abandoned cottage in hopes of seeing a raccoon that protected a ghost child. And while she was at it, she'd see if she could find indication of another dead person.

The weather was warmer than when she and Marty had staged his cottage photo op, so more people were on the trail. As usual, mostly tourists, so she didn't expect to see anyone she knew.

When she neared the cottage, she bent to tie the laces on her hiking boot. She let two college-age men walk past, and when she didn't see anyone else, she stepped off the path and quickly moved to a side of the cottage not visible from the path.

She stood amid the brush and listened to the sounds of the woods. A nearby tree frog had been disturbed and emitted rhythmic chirps. A bird, maybe a blue jay, responded to each chirp.

For more than a minute she did a slow turn. The large Halloway house was half-hidden among the pines. When maples were fully leafed, it would be hard to see one house from the other.

Muted voices came from the path. Digger reminded herself that it was a thin trail when Samantha and Cherry lived here.

The former driveway that went from the cottage to the larger house had been almost totally overgrown. She could tell from the absence of low-hanging branches that someone kept it at least passable, probably to be able to check on the cottage.

As she finished her turn, a rustle in the brush gave her a start. The raccoon stared up at her from less than three feet away.

"Okay, this is really creepy." She went to one knee, and it held her gaze. "You want to know if your friend is coming back? I guess I should bring her to see you." She realized she was whispering and smiled to herself.

As she stood, the raccoon turned and darted under a balsam fir tree. At least it hadn't hissed.

Digger sighed. She wished she knew what she was looking for. Certainly not a log with another ghost, but something had to be here.

She walked to the side of the cottage and scanned for the log she had placed a foot on, prompting Cherry to look out and be visible to Uncle Benjamin. She found it and nudged it with the toe of her boot. Nothing happened.

Digger stopped to peer into the log. She expected twigs, leaves, maybe even moss. But the interior wood was smooth, almost as if it had been sanded. A few feet in sat a flat rock. Had it been a pillow for Cherry?

What she didn't find were fragments of a child's clothes. Would they have survived for twelve years? Not intact, but she had hoped for a metal barrette or Barbie doll. At least a plastic arm or leg.

DIGGER WARMED UP SOME vegetable soup for lunch and ate at the kitchen table. She knew Uncle Benjamin would join her eventually. She tried to imagine spending all day with an eight-year-old and couldn't. It would be one thing for a parent and child to go through the routine of a school day or busy weekend, but all day alone in a house?

Bitsy trotted over and laid his head on her shoe.

"Sorry, it's vegetarian vegetable, not beef. You wouldn't want the green beans."

He plopped on his side so Digger leaned down to rub his belly.

As she dried her dishes, Uncle Benjamin floated into the kitchen. *"Cherry and Ragdoll are playing dress-up."*

"She dresses the cat?"

"She thinks she does. That's what counts. More important, Ragdoll stays with her, so she's content. Did you find anything near the cottage?"

Digger sat at the table again and Uncle Benjamin adopted his cross-legged position atop it. "I saw the raccoon and checked out her log. It's oddly clean inside."

"Makes sense to me, if she stayed in there all the time."

Digger didn't ask how a weightless ghost could have kept out sticks and moss. "I say let's head up there this afternoon. Unless you think she'll start to fade again."

Uncle Benjamin shook his head. *"I think I'm her anchor, or whatever you want to call it, at least for now. Maybe you are, too."*

Digger stood. "Great. Don't you get lost in the woods. I won't know what to do with her."

AS DIGGER PULLED HER Jeep into the parking lot at the trailhead below Old Knob, she eyed the increasingly cloudy sky. She didn't want to be climbing up, or down for that matter, on a rain-slick trail.

She put the Jeep in park and listened as Uncle Benjamin told Cherry where they were. He looked at Digger. *"Cherry is sitting very still, looking around."*

Digger busied herself with putting her keys in her purse and pretending to check for something in the glove box. She didn't want to get ahead of her ghostly pair.

After almost a minute, Cherry apparently started asking Uncle Benjamin questions. Digger watched him nod, then respond.

"I think it used to be a smaller parking lot, but more people wanted to come here, so they made it bigger."

A pause, then, *"It's still the back way to your cottage. Excuse me, your house."*

Digger opened her car door.

Uncle Benjamin nodded again. *"Digger wants to start walking up the path. Would you like to come?"* Another pause. *"I don't know the other way. I think this is fine."*

Digger glanced around. Only four cars sat in the lot, and no one was nearby. "Come on, Cherry. I think there's a chance we'll see Big Eyes."

Behind her, Uncle Benjamin said, *"Okay, wait for me! She's run ahead. I'll catch up to her."*

Digger walked at a steady pace, barely keeping Uncle Benjamin within sight. Cherry must have stopped because she caught up to him after a minute.

"I told Cherry I needed to rest." He looked down. *"Yes, Digger's a lot younger than I am."*

From above them on the trail, voices drifted down. It sounded like three or four people. Digger looked toward Uncle Benjamin's waist. "Cherry, I'm going to walk some more. You can walk with me if Uncle Benjamin wants to rest, but remember, I can't hear you."

"She says okay, she's going to go ahead of you." Uncle Benjamin walked next to Digger. *"I'm not really tired. I wanted you to catch up."*

"Sure. Is she far ahead of us?"

"Twenty yards or so. She's puzzled about how wide the tail is, but she's really excited."

Four people appeared ahead of them on the path. Digger recognized one as a man who worked at the post office, but didn't know the others. Uncle Benjamin walked past her.

The group drew closer. "Hello, Gus, isn't it?"

The older man smiled. "You're Digger, right?"

"Yes." She stopped, and the two men and two women stayed about ten feet from her farther up the trail. "Good day for some exercise."

"Sure is." He introduced his wife, Susan, and the other two, who were members of her family visiting from New England. "I keep telling them we even get some sap from these trees."

After another awkward thirty seconds, Digger let them walk past her down the trail. Gus called back, "I think you'll have The Knob to yourself."

"Sounds good." She trudged toward where she'd seen Uncle Benjamin leave the path ahead of her. As she got closer, his excited tone reached her.

"I see him, Cherry. He's happy to see you, too."

She walked off the path near the cottage and saw the raccoon standing on its hind legs, front paws resting on what she'd come to think of as Cherry's log. The animal was smelling the air.

Uncle Benjamin stood a few feet from the raccoon, mouth slightly agape. He turned to face Digger. *"They're rubbing noses."*

Digger stood next to him. "I can't believe this. It's nuts."

The raccoon dropped to all fours and waddled toward the cottage.

"He's following her," Uncle Benjamin said. *"I've been worried about her realizing no one is in the cottage."*

Digger sat on the log and watched Uncle Benjamin follow Cherry. She didn't want to be drawn into a conversation she couldn't really participate in. And in case someone else came up the path, she didn't want to appear to be talking to a tree.

She took a swig of water from the small bottle in her fanny pack and stared at the cottage. What happened to Samantha Halloway? Did Cherry have a suppressed memory of her mother being killed or carted off while the child watched from her hiding place?

After several minutes, Uncle Benjamin floated over to sit next to her. *"Was that No Trespassing sign in front of the cottage this morning?"*

"What? No." Digger stood.

Uncle Benjamin frowned. *"You should probably stay over here. The raccoon won't get prosecuted. You might."*

Digger sat next to him. "I guess I didn't prowl every inch of the area, but I think I would have noticed it."

"Looks like someone just dug the hole for a narrow dowel and stapled one of those cheap signs. Like I used to sell at the hardware store."

"Maybe because of the article in the paper "What's she doing?"

He nodded ahead of him. *"She seems to understand all this a lot better than I thought she would. She's telling Big Eyes where her bedroom was and where the TV sat in the front room. She hasn't asked why it's boarded up."*

"She hasn't asked where her mother is?"

"Not so far." He nodded toward the larger house, just visible through the trees. *"Sometime we need to come up here when I can float around in there. Makes more sense as an Underground Railroad stop than any other place for miles."*

"Because of its size?"

"Partly. Remote location. Big cellar. Some houses up here were closer to underground streams. Ground is soggier."

"So where do we go from here? About Cherry, I mean."

Uncle Benjamin shook his head. *"I have no idea. I...Cherry, stay where I can see you."*

Digger grinned. "It's not like she could trip over a tree root and hurt herself."

The raccoon had begun to amble back toward where Uncle Benjamin and Digger sat.

"Nuts. She's upset that he isn't staying with her. She's coming this way." He moved away.

Digger stood. The late afternoon air felt a lot cooler than when the sun was high, and she shivered. She'd hoped Cherry would perhaps wander to a place where she'd last seen her mother and miraculously a maternal ghost would appear who would want to care for her daughter.

Uncle Benjamin's frustration was clear. *"I'm sure he does like you, but Big Eyes may need to go somewhere else. We can see him again."*

Digger became aware of raindrops hitting the leaves above her. Cool and wet. Not a good combination, especially since the leaves weren't yet full. She glanced to the path. No one there. "Come on, Cherry. It's about to rain."

Uncle Benjamin held out a hand for her and spoke in a soothing tone. *"We'll think about how to let Big Eyes know you like him extra special much."*

As Digger turned toward the path, she heard what she thought was more rain hitting leaves or pine needles above her. But it came from about twenty yards away, in a spot where the pine trees stood more thickly.

She gasped. A thin-shouldered person, she thought a woman, had moved quickly away. All Digger could see was a blue watch cap with long brown hair streaming from it, and a navy-blue cable sweater.

What had the person overhead, and why wouldn't she show herself?

CHAPTER SEVENTEEN

WHEN DIGGER PULLED INTO the Ancestral Sanctuary drive, Franklin's Volvo sat in front of the house.

Uncle Benjamin woke Cherry, who had been napping in the Jeep's back seat. "My son is here! Cherry, you can meet Digger's cousin."

Digger loved to see Franklin, but now she would have input from two ghosts when she tried to talk to her cousin.

She smiled as she hugged him. "I didn't know you were coming. I would have cooked something special."

He released her and they walked arm-in-arm up the front steps. "I went to the law office for a couple hours this morning, but some plans I had for this evening fell through. I hopped in the car and came up here for the rest of the weekend."

"Terrific."

Behind them, Uncle Benjamin answered Cherry's questions about how old Franklin was, where he lived, and whether he brought any pets with him. Digger tried to ignore him.

"Are you and Marty doing anything tonight?"

There it was again. Franklin liked Marty, which was good, but she obviously couldn't tell him why they didn't spend more time together. "He's working on a couple stories, so I don't think so."

"On a Saturday night?"

"During the day, mostly, but he needs to chill." She hoped Franklin didn't run into Marty if he went into town. She hated to tell lies, but if she tried to explain more, Franklin would spot all the holes.

"I put your ancient tea kettle on, and I brought some wine because I know you like to mix it."

Digger said she wanted to change out of hiking clothes and made her way upstairs. Cherry seemed to continue to pepper Uncle Benjamin with questions about Franklin, because she could hear him murmuring responses.

She had to get her mind wrapped around having someone else in the house full-time. For the weekend, anyway. She changed from jeans into lighter-weight pants and a tee-shirt that said, "Bone Digger," and went back downstairs.

Franklin sat at the kitchen table reading something on his phone. At the sound of the kettle whistle, he jumped up and poured her tea and offered her what he called a splash of burgundy.

She smiled. "I'm always big on calming beverages. You seem more energized than usual."

He finished with their mugs and sat across from her. "Actually, I'm thinking of bringing a friend up here."

Something in his tone seemed to imply he was asking permission.

"That's great!" Digger grinned. "Is this a special friend?"

He blushed slightly. "It is."

"You're so funny. I can't wait to meet her."

As Franklin opened his mouth to speak, the phone rang. She went to the wall phone. "Digger here."

"Marty here."

Her heart beat faster. "Hey. What are you up to?" A legitimate question, since she had no idea.

"I was abrupt yesterday. Sorry about that."

"I get it." Digger decided Franklin could provide neutral banter. "Franklin just surprised me with a visit. You want to come up for supper?"

"Uh, no, I think I'll wait for more family stuff until we figure out our own stuff. I'm not mad, it just…makes sense."

"I understand what you're saying."

"Is he sitting right there?"

"Yep."

"Tell him I said hello. I'll let you go."

She hung up. "He says hello. Maybe next time." She sat down. "So, tell me about your friend."

Franklin flushed again. "I think I'll surprise you."

That seemed odd, but Franklin had never dated much. From what she'd heard, he'd had a small group of high school friends. She knew he kept in touch with several of them. College and law school had been all about studying, and he seemed to take his law career in Washington, DC, very seriously. When she and Uncle Benjamin had visited him in DC, they generally ate dinner with only him, though occasionally a friend would stop at their table.

"Okay, keep your secret. Since you're here, I'm going to get stuff to make chili."

"I'll take us out."

"It's no fun to make it for just me. I'll run to town to get hamburger and some onions and cheddar cheese. I have everything else."

"If you insist. I got up at six. I might take a short walk and then lie down for a few minutes."

"We can't ride with Digger, Cherry. Plus, I want to follow my son around."

AS SHE RETURNED FROM the grocery store, Digger didn't expect to see a lone branch lying partway across the gravel. Even if the wind had blown down limbs, this one was too far from a tree to have landed there. Odd.

She stopped the Jeep and got out, careful to avoid a spot where the drive was more mud than gravel. As she stooped to grab the branch, steps behind her made her turn. If she hadn't, the tire iron the woman aimed for her shoulder probably would have broken her collar bone.

"What the hell!" She dodged and slipped to one knee as the metal rod came close enough for her to hear a whoosh. Without any conscious thought, she half-crouched and half-stood and made for the passenger side of the Jeep. When she got there, she stood fully.

The woman, perhaps ten or fifteen years older than she, followed, but Digger stayed ahead of her. In seconds they were on opposite sides of the vehicle playing a version of dodgeball, minus the ball.

"Who are you? What do you want?"

The woman's face reddened and contorted with rage. She held the tire iron at shoulder-height, like a baseball bat. "I want you to stay away!"

Digger studied the thin frame and mousy brown, shoulder-length hair. Could this be the woman from the woods near the cottage? She tried to slow her breathing. "I don't know you. You need to put down the tire iron."

"What did you do with my daughter's body?"

Digger felt her jaw drop. It seemed impossible. "You're, you're Samantha? But you're dead!"

The woman lowered the tire iron so that it hung at her side. The flush left her face and her eyes, which had been bright with anger, stared sullenly. "Only on the inside." She brought the tire iron back up, but it was clearly an effort. "Where did you put her?"

"Samantha, I was in middle school when you disappeared. I didn't know her."

She lowered the tire iron to her side and stared. "You said her name. Today by the cottage, you said her name."

"Where have you been? You stayed here all this time?"

She leaned against the car and the tire iron clattered to the ground. "I didn't...I ran. Far away." She put her head on the car hood. "It's my fault she died." Her thin shoulders heaved with dry sobs.

Digger stayed still for several seconds, then glanced toward the house. No sign of Franklin. Uncle Benjamin didn't appear either, which meant Cherry probably couldn't see her mother. "Samantha. Listen."

The woman didn't raise her head.

"Samantha, it's important. I can help you, but not right here, right now." She had a thought. "Get in my car, back it out of the drive and wait along the road. About thirty yards down, there's a place where you can park. I'll be there in a few minutes."

She raised her head. "You're going to call the sheriff and say I stole your car."

Digger smiled in spite of her confusion. "No. I'll be there in five minutes. Ten. I need to tell my uncle where I'm going."

Her look of suspicion increased. "He'll call the sheriff."

Digger shook her head. "Not if he knows where I am. If I don't show up, he might. The keys are in the ignition." She turned and continued up the drive, stooping to pick up the branch and move it to one side.

After about fifteen seconds, the ignition turned over. Digger looked over her shoulder to be sure Samantha backed up rather than barreled forward to run her over. Digger had the presence of mind to wonder where Samantha had parked her car.

She quickened her pace, but remembered she didn't have her house keys. "Damn it." Maybe the back door was open. As she neared the house. Ragdoll hopped on the table in front of the window, and Digger remembered she'd left the window unlocked. "Small favors."

She jogged up the steps. She didn't want to wake Franklin and hoped he was napping in his third-floor apartment and not the living room.

As she grasped the window frame at the bottom, Ragdoll meowed and hopped off the table. The window rose easily, and she felt glad the screen was raised.

"What are you doing? Did you forget your keys?"

Digger reached in, grabbed the lamp from the table, and sat it on the floor. "More or less. Too bad you can't flip a lock."

"Yes, Cherry, she's being very silly."

Digger slid the table a couple feet to the right, swung her right leg over the frame, and let herself fall gently onto the living room floor. Bitsy placed both paws on her chest and licked her face.

Uncle Benjamin and Cherry stood near her, holding hands. *"You should hide a key."*

She gently pushed Bitsy aside as she patted his head, stood, and closed the window. "You did, but I had the locks changed because half the people you knew could find the one you hid."

"Where's your car?"

"Lent it to…a friend. It'll be back soon."

Uncle Benjamin studied her. *"Have you been smoking some wacky tobaccy?"*

"Feels like it." She regarded his hand that held Cherry's. "Cherry, I think I scared Ragdoll. Could you see if she's okay?"

Uncle Benjamin turned his head, apparently following her progress toward the staircase, and then met Digger's eyes. *"What is going on?"*

Digger crossed to the sofa and sat. She leaned back and shut her eyes for a moment. "You won't believe this." Bitsy bounded onto her lap and nuzzled her chin. "Oof. You are not a lap dog," She patted his head.

"I never would have believed you'd come in the porch window, so try me."

She opened her eyes, met his, and whispered, "Samantha's alive."

"Alive, alive?" He gestured down the front of his Peter Pan outfit. *"Not like me?"*

"I doubt she'd be caught dead or alive in that outfit. She's in my Jeep, parked along the road."

"You're sure it's her?"

"Pretty sure." She stood and Bitsy bounded to the floor. "I wanted you to know where I am. I'm going to go talk to her."

"You can't go alone. I should…" He glanced toward the hallway. *"I'm glad you found her. Under your bed because she likes you."* His gaze followed Cherry up the steps and returned to Digger. *"Maybe you should wake Franklin."*

"He doesn't even know about you. I can't get into Cherry and Samantha."

Uncle Benjamin frowned. *"Are you going to bring her back here?"*

Digger shook her head. They both realized they couldn't bring Samantha into the Ancestral Sanctuary until they figured out some things. And, Digger thought, make sure she doesn't bring her tire iron. Though she didn't say that to Uncle Benjamin. "I'm going to feed Bitsy and grab a couple waters."

As Digger made her way to the kitchen, Uncle Benjamin followed Cherry up the stairs. *"Let's see if we can get Ragdoll to come out from under your bed."*

Digger poured a double helping of food into each animal's bowl and made sure they had enough water for the evening.

She scribbled a note for Franklin and left it on the kitchen table. "Had to help a friend for a few minutes. Back soon."

She grabbed the water and took two apples from the crisper and ran down the back steps. She slowed to a walk on the driveway.

Where had Samantha been? Close by? But that made no sense. Did she read the *Maple Grove News* online? Had she read Marty's Friday article and decided to check on her old cottage? Did her father know she was alive?

The latter thought made Digger furious. How could someone worry their family and friends for so long? Or was she running from someone she knew?

She finally reached the end of the long driveway and turned right. The road rose slowly and veered slightly to the left. Her Jeep came into view, but no woman sat in the driver's seat. "Damn."

As she got closer to the car, Digger softly called Samantha's name. She scanned the woods alongside the road. Two pink dogwoods sat among the mix of maple, oak, and pine trees. But no thin woman with dull eyes and mousy brown hair.

Digger walked around the Jeep and looked on both sides of the narrow road. She sighed and put the two bottles of water and apples behind a bush. "If you're here, have an apple. We need to talk. But it's really, really important that you not come to my house."

She climbed into the Jeep, thankful Samantha had left the keys in the ignition, and drove a few hundred yards up the road until she got to a spot wide enough to turn around.

As she approached the area where Samantha had parked the Jeep, the woman stepped onto the road holding the two apples, with a bottle of water in each pocket of her jacket.

Digger slowed to a stop and Samantha walked around the Jeep and slid into the front passenger seat. "My car is in the small overlook higher up the mountain. You can head that way."

"Okay." Digger traveled the short distance to the Ancestral Sanctuary driveway, drove in a few feet, and backed onto the road again.

Samantha bit into the apple. "Thanks. I had a long drive to get here."

"You're welcome." Digger had a dozen questions, but she said nothing as she turned into the small lot by the overlook and parked next to a battered-looking gold Honda Civic with New Jersey plates. For several seconds, the two women looked ahead to the lush valley below and the taller mountain behind it.

Samantha turned her head toward Digger. "You sounded as if you were talking to my daughter, but she's dead."

"I can explain, but can I ask you a couple questions first?"

"No."

Digger sighed deeply. "You're going to have a hard time accepting what I tell you."

"Nothing can be harder than losing a child."

"I suppose not. Do you believe in ghosts?"

"No."

Digger studied a pink dogwood that stood behind the thick wall of stones that separated the narrow parking spaces from the side of the mountain. "Then we should probably stop talking."

Samantha turned her head sharply, to face Digger's profile. "What the hell is that supposed to mean?"

Digger stared ahead. "It means that when my uncle died last year, the day they buried him his ghost popped up in the kitchen in the house he left me. And he can see other ghosts. Or some of them, anyway." She thought about the woman he'd seen from a distance when they visited a coal museum in Kitzmiller last year. He hadn't mentioned more ghosts, but maybe he'd seen others before Cherry.

"That's a load of bull." Samantha's face reddened again. "What are you trying to do? Convince my father she's alive or something?"

"So, he told you I met him on Friday?"

"I haven't spoken to my father since the night he tried to strangle me twelve years ago."

"Good God. Is that why Cherry was hiding in the log?"

In less than a second, Samantha bent at the waist and covered her face with her hands, sobbing.

Digger listened to the deep sobs for almost a minute before placing a hand on her shoulder. "I'm really sorry I upset you." She pulled back her hand, then reached into the compartment between the bucket seats and took out a couple of fast-food napkins, which she placed on Samantha's left knee.

Samantha took them and turned her head toward the passenger door as she blew her nose and wiped her eyes. Then she straightened and stared out the passenger window. "How did you know about the log?"

"I hiked up there last weekend with a friend who wanted to take pictures of the cottage and…"

"Pictures? For God's sake, why?"

"He takes hundreds a year, so do I, of anything that looks interesting or different." She decided not to say Marty was the reporter who wrote the most recent article.

Samantha shuddered. "I hadn't seen it in more than a decade. I thought it would have fallen down by now."

"Does, uh, anyone know you're alive?"

She shook her head. "I'm listening, not talking."

"Okay. My uncle went with us, Uncle Benjamin. But my friend can't see him. It's…hard." Her throat tightened and she cleared it. "The only ghost I can see is my uncle, but he could see Cherry. She…her ghost looked up at us from a hollow log."

Silent tears rolled down Samantha's cheeks.

"Anyway, I guess she was weak. My uncle scooped her up and ran for my car. She's, uh, living in my house with him."

Samantha's neck almost snapped as she faced Digger. "Are you telling me that my ghost daughter lives in your house, and you talk to her?"

"I don't. Uncle Benjamin does. He tells me what she says."

Samantha turned back to the passenger window. "But you called to her when you were at the cottage."

"She can see and hear me. I had no link with her when she was alive, so maybe that's why I can't see her."

In a flat tone, Samantha said, "I don't believe you."

"I guess that's easier, in a way. If you came with me and she could see you, but you couldn't see her, I don't know what it would do to her."

"Like kill her?" Sarcasm oozed with the words.

"I don't know how that works. I know that Uncle Benjamin has to be with me or on the Ancestral Sanctuary property or he fades."

"He what?"

"He starts to fade away. I left him, by accident, one day, and by the time he got back to me he was almost transparent. Took him a few hours to get back to normal. Or whatever you call it."

"So, if Cherry's a ghost, why doesn't she have to stay at the cottage?"

Digger shook her head. "Uncle Benjamin thought he was the first ghost she encountered, and she kind of latched onto him. When we took her to the cottage to look for the raccoon, she…"

"I saw that creature. It leaned on the log I hid her in."

Now Digger knew for sure how Cherry got into the log. "According to Uncle Benjamin, it leaned on the log because Cherry was on the other side of it. They rubbed noses."

Samantha stared at Digger.

Digger sighed. "I can only repeat what she told Uncle Benjamin. She didn't seem to have a good sense of time. She still looks eight and thinks she is. She said the raccoon kept her warm sometimes. In the log."

Samantha opened the car door, slid out, and slammed it. As she walked to her car, she yelled, "I don't believe a damn word of it!" The last words came as a sob.

Digger got out of her car but didn't follow her. "I don't blame you. But if you want to talk more, call my cell." She gave the number. "If you want to try to see Cherry, Uncle Benjamin will have to prepare her."

She glanced at the license plate. The last two digits were smeared in mud, probably deliberate. She committed the first part to memory.

Samantha yanked open her car door. "There's no such thing as ghosts." She got in the car and turned the ignition. She backed up in two jerky motions and passed in front of Digger.

Digger turned to open her car door, but Samantha backed up until her car sat beside Digger. She rolled down her window. "Are you trying to con my old man out of money?"

Digger frowned. "Of course not. If I told this story to anyone else, I'd get committed."

Samantha stared, her face impassive. "He's a cheap bastard. Take him for all he's worth."

CHAPTER EIGHTEEN

BACK AT THE ANCESTRAL Sanctuary, Digger found an agitated Uncle Benjamin floating around the living room. *"What would I have done if you hadn't come back?"*

"I was just down the road."

His eyes went toward the hallway staircase. *"Yes, Cherry, she's home. I'll be up in a minute."* He faced Digger. *"I told her I had to wait for you down here."*

Digger bent to scratch Bitsy's head. "In a minute, Boy." She looked at Uncle Benjamin and lowered her voice. "Definitely Samantha, but she didn't believe me."

"The heck you say. Where has she been?"

"The tags on the car she drove were from New Jersey, but I don't know if that's where she lives. She thinks I'm trying to con her father or something."

"Makes no sense to me. Why would she stay away?"

Digger shook her head. She felt emotionally drained. "Would you believe our story?"

Uncle Benjamin shook his head slowly. *"How did Cherry get in that log?"* His face appeared stricken as he looked toward the bottom of the stairs. *"Cherry must have tiptoed down the stairs. She reminds me that she and her mommy played hide and seek, and she fell asleep."*

How long had Cherry been there? Digger smiled toward the steps. "I'm going to take Bitsy for a walk. You want to come?"

"She says you have poop to clean up near the back porch steps." Uncle Benjamin grinned broadly in Cherry's direction. *"I'm so glad you reminded her."*

"Yes, thanks, Cherry." She bowed slightly, gesturing Uncle Benjamin up the steps. "You can have a good game of hide and seek, too."

He scowled and followed Cherry up the stairs.

Digger headed to the kitchen. She'd brought her groceries in but left them on the floor in the hall. She carried them to the kitchen, dumped the hamburger in a skillet, and turned the stove on low.

Because she didn't want to hear more about Bitsy's droppings, she opened the back door and let him into the yard. He wouldn't run into the woods when she was out with him. As she deposited a bag into the outdoor trash can, her cell phone rang.

A blocked number. She started to ignore the call but thought better of it. "Yes."

Samantha's tone was strident. "I'm not saying I believe you, but what if I did?"

"I don't think I'm the one to convince you. Even if you can't see her, Uncle Benjamin could tell you what she says. You could ask her something we wouldn't know."

"Like what?"

"How would I...okay. She talks about somebody she calls "the Yeller." Who was that?"

The phone clicked and Digger swore to herself. "What a stupid thing to ask her."

She walked up the small rise into the Browning family plot and stood in front of Uncle Benjamin's headstone. "What if I really am imagining all of this?"

No, she couldn't be. She hadn't known who Samantha or Cherry were. The cottage was real, they had lived there. Cherry had died near there, and Uncle Benjamin had found her.

Digger stared at each of the twelve headstones, many unreadable. Most would have been lost to time if Uncle Benjamin and his parents hadn't kept them standing and patched some of them.

The Halloway property had been in that family for generations. But she didn't recall mention of them in local history books. Since she had helped develop the historical society's index, Digger knew the Halloways didn't have an individual family history in the society's collection.

A lot of people didn't care about their ancestors, but in Maple Grove, longtime families usually did. Maybe Samantha and Cherry weren't the only missing leaves on the family tree.

Digger sighed and turned back toward the house. She wanted to see what information she could find about Samantha in New Jersey. If she talked to Sheriff Montgomery, he could look for New Jersey license plates with the partial number she could give him. But he might also call Franklin to say he should check her into a hospital.

AFTER THE DINNER OF chili and an apple cobbler Franklin whipped up, Digger took her laptop to the living room couch and Franklin sat in the comfortable upholstered chair to read.

She lay down with the computer on her stomach. Of course, there was no Samantha Halloway in New Jersey. No S. Halloway or Samantha Hall.

She thought the initial flyer about the disappearance had a middle name, so she pulled it up. Samantha Marie Halloway. She tried variations of the full name and checked public records for marriages. Nothing.

"Digger."

She started and looked at her cousin.

"You must really be into that family history stuff. I said your name twice."

She switched the tab to another one, so if he came to the couch Franklin wouldn't see Samantha's information. "I get way too focused. What's up?"

"Nothing. I was thinking if we're sitting in the same room, it's weird not to talk."

Digger sat up. "Tell me more about your friend."

"Oh, jeez. Go back to your research. I'm not ready for that." In an exaggerated motion, he pretended to hide behind the cover of his book.

"You're reading *Pompeii* by Robert Harris? Don't you kind of know the ending?"

He stayed behind the book. "Do your thing."

"Okay. I think there was a volcano involved."

He laughed and looked over the top of the book. "Dig up some more modern history."

"If you insist." Digger had a subscription to digital newspaper files and checked that. Eventually she found an S. Marie Hall in Ocean Alley. The small Jersey Shore town ran along the ocean for more than a mile and seemed to be only a few blocks deep. S. Marie Hall was captioned in a photo of staff for a daycare center that had opened ten years earlier.

Digger studied the grainy photo. The woman was white and about the right age. Average height and weight. But it was impossible to identify facial features.

She closed the laptop. After hiking up the mountain twice she was tired and decided to take a hot bath and go to bed.

Uncle Benjamin floated into the room. *"She finally went to sleep. She must have mentioned that raccoon ten times."*

Digger glanced at Franklin, who nodded into his book. "Sleepy head."

"Oh, right." He straightened. "It's so relaxing here I always sleep more."

"I'd give anything to be able to talk to him."

Digger wanted to tell him she thought Franklin would say the same. Maybe someday.

FRANKLIN LEFT EARLIER THAN usual on Sunday.

Digger walked to his car and handed him a plastic bowl with a big piece of cobbler in it. "Leaving so early hardly makes the drive seem worth it."

"My batteries are recharged." He took the bowl and gave her a quick hug. "Tell Marty next time he doesn't get off so easy."

"I'm pretty sure he doesn't think anything about me is easy." She stood on the porch until Franklin had gone all the way down the drive and turned onto the road.

Bitsy whimpered from the front hallway, so she opened the door. "Don't go chasing after squirrels or I'll make you take a bath."

She stood in the front hall and tried to see the house as Franklin's friend would. She'd bought paint for the hallway and living room. The living room would take ages, but she could use the ivory color in the hall. It'd be a lot better than the current dark tan. The space had a dingy air.

Digger spent as much time taping the wooden baseboards and chair rail as she did painting the walls. At the end of three hours, she had a stiff neck and a much brighter hallway. She drank iced tea and examined the paint under her fingernails. "Oh, well."

Cherry and Uncle Benjamin had watched her several times, but she had finally asked if Bitsy could go into the yard so Cherry could play with him. Digger shut the door behind the dog.

Uncle Benjamin stood next to Digger and looked outside. *"Did you think everything was okay with Franklin?"*

"Sure. Didn't you think so?"

"I kept thinking he had something to tell you."

Digger grinned. "I think he wanted to tell me about a girlfriend. He decided to bring her up to introduce us. Well, me."

Uncle Benjamin's delighted smile faded. *"You think we should tell him?"*

Digger thought about how Marty acted when she did what she called zoning out. "Probably, but not when he has a new girlfriend here."

AFTER LUNCH, DIGGER PULLED out her research folders on Holly's family and opened her laptop. She sat at the dining room table so her aching muscles wouldn't beg for a nap on the couch.

First, she found the pages she'd taken pictures of at the historical society and printed them. The handwriting had faded since the latter part of the nineteenth century, but she could make out most of it.

She went first to the one by Bessie, which was a nickname for Elizabeth. If Digger understood the flow, the woman's recollections had been written many years after the events she recorded. The first of several pages she had copied were titled, **"The Night We Were Almost Cot."**

Clouds was supposed to cover the moon better. When we got just above the railroad, it come out and we had to stay in the bushes.

I heared people a ways down the tracks. I thought mebbe they were looking to catch Negros. Because of the reward money.

Then the train got closer. I told the old woman we had to move, but she was real slow. The train always go slow near town, but I knew she wasn't going to make it. I waved and one of the Union men, he climbed down and he grab her. The other man take her and then the first man jump back on the train.

Then I heared shouting heading toward town, and I run up the mountain as fast as I could.

That old woman was probly in Pennsylvania by sun-up. I was proud of me. Pride is a sin, but that woman wouldn't be free if I didn't take her down the mountain to the train.

Digger reread the passage and glanced again at the date on the small volume. April 5, 1878. Because of the date, whoever catalogued it hadn't realized one of the stories dealt with clandestine help for escaping slaves.

If Union Troops were on the train, it had to be during the Civil War. Probably supply trains. The short piece was an historical treasure.

Down the mountain? If it was in the Maple Grove Historical Society, it almost had to be Meadow Mountain. There were two distinct clusters of families on the mountain during the Civil War. One small group on the western side, where the Halloway house still stood, included the Hurder family and several others.

From there it would have been possible to trek down the mountain to the rails. Assuming it wasn't one of the times that Confederate raiders blew up tracks further southeast of Maple Grove.

Bessie's story made Digger more certain that there had been Underground Railroad activity on the mountain. And could Bessie have been Elizabeth Washington? It would take more research to know for sure, but it was at least a possibility.

Maybe Holly's Grandmother Audrey would know. She wasn't a Washington by birth, but surely she and her husband had talked about where their families were during that time.

Digger sighed and opened her computer. She had posted more information on Holly's family on Ancestry. At least what she thought the correct family lines were. She hadn't expected any messages so quickly, but one had come early that morning. "Six AM. Early for a Sunday."

Because she managed Holly's DNA information, the man had sent a note to Digger, assuming she was Holly. Digger read with amazement.

"My name is Daniel Michael Washington, and I live in Pittsburgh. I think we may be related. I'm descended from Charles Washington and Elizabeth Hurder, who lived in what is now Garrett County, Maryland. I believe you descend from their son Jeremiah. I am from their son Abraham. I'd like to exchange more information. I've recently been in contact with another distant cousin who has a photo of Charles and Elizabeth. I'd like to see if it matches anything you have."

He gave an email address, but before she responded, Digger clicked on a link that led her to his family tree. His ancestors were largely from West

Virginia and Maryland, which meant just across the Potomac River from each other. The only pictures showed African American lineage.

Digger penned a reply. She explained she was not Holly, but a friend gathering family data. She outlined the census information she had on the Hurder family, and asked if he knew who Elizabeth's parents were.

His tactful reply named "Lawrence Hurder as the father, but Elizabeth's mother is uncertain." He looked forward to exploring that with Holly.

Digger stared at his words. She knew from her own work that the Hurder family was white. If Elizabeth Washington had ancestors in that family, her pedigree was definitely a blended portion of the melting pot.

CHAPTER NINETEEN

DIGGER FELT ANXIOUS MONDAY morning. She wasn't sure how to talk to Holly about the probable family connection, and Marty didn't want to spend time with her family until she and he "figured out their own stuff." Or something like that.

She and Holly role-played a conversation they planned to have with Gene and Abigail at the chamber office the next day. Because their proposal would involve Gene spending some money, it wouldn't be easy.

Their job was to show Gene that the chamber could bring in revenue selling the calendars Digger and Holly would do for them. Starting early would garner interest as they took photos of various businesses over several months. Everyone wanted to see glossy pictures of their stores or companies.

Digger kept expecting the phone to ring with Samantha saying she had decided to believe Digger's information about Cherry, and could she please see her ghost daughter. "Dream on," she muttered.

Holly's tone sounded concerned. "Digger? You okay?"

"Oh, sure. Just thinking out loud." She glanced at Holly. "What?"

"Oh, nothing…Well, maybe nothing." She stood and walked to Digger's desk. "I ran into Marty in the grocery store on Sunday. He sounded almost worried about you."

"Worried?"

Holly frowned. "You don't play dumb well. He asked if I thought the stress of your Uncle Benjamin's death was getting to you more now. He asked if you stared into space a lot."

Digger pretended to see humor in his questions. "I've accused him of being a space cadet when he's thinking about what he's writing."

"Zoned out. He asked if I thought you zoned out sometimes."

Now it didn't seem funny at all. Marty didn't need to talk to people about her mental health. "I'll have to get him to take me to lunch or something. I can pretend to stare at everyone else in the room."

Holly raised an eyebrow. "You're evading something. Tell me whenever you want to."

DIGGER PULLED OPEN THE glass door to the newspaper office on Monday afternoon. If she didn't tell Marty now, she never would. Forget ghosts. Would he even believe that she had seen the living Samantha Marie Holloway?

Marty stood behind the counter, leaning on it. Across from him stood Uncle Benjamin's old friend Thelma Zorn, and they had their heads closer together than two people normally would. The phrase "deep in conversation" came to mind.

Both turned toward her. Thelma looked surprised, but smiled broadly. Marty didn't.

"Digger, it's so good to see you. I thought you'd be back to sift for more Underground Railroad materials."

Digger held up a hand, which showed white and beige paint spatters. "I've been painting in the house, now that it's warm enough to open the windows."

"I can't wait to see all you've done to brighten up that old house."

"Come by anytime." She looked at Marty. "I can come back."

Thelma shook her head. "I'm done. I brought Marty copies of pages from the scrapbooks." She lowered her voice. "About the Halloway disappearances." She took her purse from where it sat on the counter. "I have chicken in the crock pot."

Digger noted several photocopies had been under the purse. "Sounds good." She waited until the door's bell tinkled and looked at Marty. "Can we talk in your office for a minute?"

"Sure." He picked up the papers and called over his shoulder. "Anna, I'm off the desk for a minute."

He pointed to his office at the far end, across from the counter. "Come on back."

Digger followed him into his cluttered space. Unlike other times she been there, the piles of file folders were not neatly stacked and two empty mugs sat on the credenza behind his desk. Its piles of old newspapers and folders were also haphazardly arrayed.

As he leaned against his desk, Marty's eyes had followed her gaze. "Yes, my office is a mess. What did you want to say?"

She took a breath, then let her eyes wander to a tall bookshelf, the four-drawer file cabinet, and the window.

"Digger I don't have time for…"

"He's a ghost." She talked very fast, afraid she would stop. "He found her in a log. The raccoon always stayed with her. That's why it hissed at us. She doesn't know about her mother. She was really faded, but she's…"

Marty held up a hand, palm toward her. "You're talking gibberish."

She leaned against the wall. Her shoulder blade turned off the light switch, so she turned and flipped it back on and took a deep breath. "Uncle Benjamin came back the day of his funeral. He can go anywhere on the Ancestral Sanctuary property or go with me. He can't go anywhere else." She leaned into the wall and shut her eyes. When she opened them, Marty hadn't moved.

"Say something, damn it."

He straightened his shoulders and sat the file folder he'd carried on his desk. "Hard to know how to respond. You mean the raccoon next to the cottage?"

"Not about the raccoon. He's still alive. About Uncle Benjamin!"

He walked toward her, and Digger wondered if he was going to turn her around and point to the door. Instead, he reached past her and shut it. "Have a seat, Digger."

He took a pile of old papers off one of the two wood chairs that sat across from his desk. He sat in the other one and angled it so he faced her. "Tell me what you're talking about."

She sat, feeling irritated now. "You know what I mean. Uncle Benjamin's ghost appeared right after the last shovel of dirt covered his coffin. He's been with me ever since."

"I guess I …I knew what you were going to say. Now I have to figure out if I believe it."

Digger could feel her face reddening. "If you weren't going to believe me, why did you try to drag it out of me?"

"I wasn't trying…I don't know how to react." His voice softened. "I want to believe you."

She did an exaggerated shrug. "It's not like I can prove it to you. You either believe it or you don't."

He wet his lips. "Okay. I do." He grinned. "Not that 'I do,' I mean I believe you."

It was probably the only thing he could have said to make her smile. She leaned across the chair to hug him, keeping her eyes tightly closed. If she opened them, she knew she'd cry.

He held her and put his chin on top of her head. "So, he haunts the place, huh? Do ghosts give hugs?"

Digger slapped him lightly on his upper arm. "He doesn't haunt. It's like he's still alive. Except he's not. And you're a dork."

"Thank you."

They pulled apart, and she stared into his eyes, which seemed to be a deeper brown than usual. "It's very hard to be…personal when he's around."

Marty snorted. "Thanks for the warning."

She wiped a finger under each eye where two tears of relief had leaked out. "He stays at the house, on the property, or with me. Sometimes we could go to your place."

He grinned. "Or have a romantic weekend."

She smiled and nodded, then her smile faded. "But first, we have to figure out about Cherry."

He sat back and his face became impassive. "The little girl. Hamil Halloway's granddaughter?"

Anna knocked on his door. "Marty, are you taking calls?"

He stood and opened the door. "Sorry. Didn't mean to be secretive."

Digger called, "Hi, Anna."

"Hey, Digger." To Marty, she said, "Mayor Westlake's on the phone. He thinks you should mind your own business."

"What else is new? Did he say about what?"

From down the hall, Wendell Hines yelled, "About that damn Halloway story."

Marty winked at Anna and raised his voice. "How many more papers did you sell that day?"

"Heh, heh, heh." Hines didn't say more.

"Put the mayor in here, would you, Anna?"

She grinned. "With pleasure." She started to pull the door shut.

"You can leave it open." Marty went behind his desk, stayed standing, and placed his hand above the receiver. He looked at Digger. "This'll just take a minute. He needs to vent."

The phone rang and he picked it up. "Mr. Mayor." He listened for several seconds. "Uh huh. Really." More listening. "Okay. I get your perspective. Uh huh." He looked at Digger and made a circular motion with one finger.

She smiled and repeated it.

"Yes, sir. Will do." Marty hung up. He frowned. "Bunch of kids went up there and put graffiti on The Knob. He's blaming the story."

"Story might have drawn their attention. They did the drawings."

"Wish I'd thought to say that. Halloway called him, really mad. He's worried somebody'll try to get into the cottage."

Digger drew a breath. "I should go."

He nodded. "Can I come out there tonight about seven?"

"You sure you want to?"

He sat in his desk chair. "It's all weird. But you usually aren't. At least, you never were before you started zoning in and out of conversations. I guess this is why. We gotta talk more about it." He smiled and gestured to the door. "Go away. Before I drive my grandparents over to Frostburg for an appointment, I have to make nice with the mayor and sheriff about the graffiti."

As Digger left, she realized she hadn't told him the most important piece of information. A living Samantha Halloway would change everything.

CHAPTER TWENTY

DIGGER HAD A LOT MORE confidence in the baked salmon than in how Monday evening with Marty would go. She'd extracted a promise from Uncle Benjamin to take Cherry to the third floor to play in Franklin's apartment. At the very least, they had to stay far away from her and Marty. She didn't want to see Uncle Benjamin's shape bobbing through a wall.

Seven PM came and went, and Digger was glad she hadn't put the salmon in the oven. She had tossed the salad and now the multi-colored mix sat in the middle of the dining room table. A loaf of French bread sat waiting to be put in the oven just before she took out the salmon. All she needed was Marty.

She distracted herself by opening her email and found more information from Daniel Washington, including two photo attachments. His own showed a handsome man, and his forehead and chin brought to mind Holly's. Or was Digger grasping at anything that might help Holly accept her ancestry?

The second photo revealed Charles and Elizabeth Washington. The formal portrait was from the era when people had to pose for more than the fraction of a second that modern cameras permit. Neither smiled, but at least their lips weren't pursed.

Elizabeth was very light-skinned, with hair characteristic of African-American women. Daniel Washington's note said the photo was taken in 1885, so just one year before Charles Washington's death.

Digger sent the photo to her printer and stuck it in the green folder she used for confirmed information on Holly's family. Part of her wanted to leave the photo for Holly to find on her desk, so she could absorb the material privately. But was she thinking that way because she was unsure of Holly's reaction? A good friend would probably sit with her as she read it.

Finally, the doorbell rang at seven-fifteen. Bitsy barked and ran from the kitchen, where he'd hovered since she started cooking. Digger followed, determined not to be self-conscious. She and Marty had been friends for almost a year. She thought of him differently, but she didn't have to feel like an awkward teenager.

She waved through the glass in the front door and unlocked it. "Welcome to dinner."

He'd had one hand at his side and lifted it to show a small vase with a spray of fresh carnations. "To grace your dinner table."

Digger stood aside so he could enter and took the flowers. "Thanks. They'll look good in the dining room."

He hung up his lightweight jacket on the coat rack. "Smells good."

"That's a spicy vegetable casserole, which Bitsy thinks he wants, but he wouldn't like it. You hungry enough that I should put the salmon in the oven now?"

"Famished." He followed her through the dining room into the kitchen. As Digger placed the baking dish with fresh salmon in the oven, he glanced at the kitchen table.

She opened the fridge. "White wine? I have Riesling."

"I forgot. I have some Chardonnay in the car. I'll get it." He walked briskly down the hall and out the front door.

Uncle Benjamin's voice came from behind Digger. *"I told you Chardonnay would be better."*

"Damn it, you promised to stay upstairs!"

"I know, but I'm following Cherry. She wanted to look for Bitsy."

Digger sighed and threw up her arms. "Right now?"

Marty's voice came from the front door. "Right now what?"

Digger stood still for two or three seconds and turned to face him as he came down the hallway toward the kitchen. She glanced at the stove. "The timer isn't working. We'll have to keep track."

He frowned and walked to the stove to fiddle with the timer. "Seems okay. How long should I set it?"

"Sixteen minutes. Please."

She stared as he twisted the dial with the hand not holding the wine bottle.

He faced her, wearing the expression that said she just did something he thought odd. "Got it." He held up the bottle. "Got a corkscrew?"

She smiled and reached into the counter drawer next to the stove and extracted one. "Ready and waiting. Glasses are on the dining room table."

When he turned to go to the dining room, Digger looked all around. No sign of Uncle Benjamin. And she certainly wouldn't know if Cherry were in the room.

As she started to follow Marty, he turned abruptly and they almost collided.

"Sorry. I should open this over the sink."

She stepped to one side. "Did you take your grandparents over to Frostburg?"

He grinned. "I did. My grandfather insists one broken finger shouldn't keep him off the highway and my grandmother said she'd hide the keys if he tried. Using me kept peace in the house."

"Sounds like something Uncle Benjamin would try to do."

"*I would not.*"

Digger stiffened. She couldn't remember ever being this angry with him. She turned slowly. Uncle Benjamin looked at her, his eyes widened, and he quickly floated up the back stairway. She glanced at Marty to find him regarding her closely.

"This isn't going to be one of your weird nights, is it?"

"God, I hope not."

By the time the salmon was ready, Digger felt relaxed again. She suggested they fill their plates in the kitchen, and they ate a leisurely dinner at the huge dining room table.

"I think I'm making progress on Holly's family."

Marty looked surprised. "How? I thought I'd beaten every dead horse in the county."

"A little bit census proximity and a little bit DNA."

"Census proximity?"

"She agreed that her great, great grandfather most likely was Charles Washington. His brief will indicated his wife was Elizabeth, but you know how common that name was in the 1870s and 1880s."

"Right. Did you find a marriage record?"

"Papers weren't always filed in the county courthouse." She took a drink of wine. "I got to thinking about something Uncle Benjamin said one time, that a lot of freed slaves took the last names of their former owners."

"So, you figured out her name before she married?"

"The historical society has some records of owners who freed their slaves."

"Manumitted. You know, some slave owners did that so they didn't have to provide food and housing when it was no longer," he captioned the next word with his fingers, "profitable."

Digger nodded. "One more cruelty. Among the families I found records of were the Hurders, who lived next door to the Halloways."

"That's a weird coincidence. There wasn't any farming up there. Why did they have slaves?"

"It looks as if the Hurders were blacksmiths. I guess the male slaves did that. Maybe some other trades. Anyway, on the 1870 Census there is a multi-racial woman named Elizabeth Hurder. She wasn't on the 1850 or 1860 Censuses as Elizabeth Hurder, but a child in the slave family was in the same age group. I thought she could be a former slave who took the family's name."

"What does that prove?"

"Not much." She grinned as he regarded her over his glasses. "But I'm the one who manages Holly's DNA information, on Ancestry. There have been several inquiries, but no one knew more than Holly did about their families in the mid-1800s."

"So how does that help?"

"A man who contacted me this week, contacted Holly through me, has a DNA match that says he and Holly are third cousins. His great grandfather was Elizabeth Hurder Washington's son, Abraham. Holly is descended from Abraham's brother, Jeremiah."

Marty thought about that for a moment. "So…his great grandfather's sibling is the connection to Holly?"

"Looks like it. Charles Washington was a minister. The man who contacted me, his name's Daniel Washington, said someone else in his family had a photo of Charles with his wife." Digger had been about to show Marty the photo she'd printed, but changed her mind. Sharing the picture should be up to Holly.

"So, she could go from nothing to a name and a photograph? That's pretty amazing."

"It is. I can't wait…"

Uncle Benjamin's voice came down the back stairs. *"Cherry, we need to stay upstairs. Digger has company."*

"Can't wait for what?" Marty asked.

Digger wanted to say she couldn't wait to kill Uncle Benjamin, but that wouldn't solve anything. "I just had a thought."

From the kitchen, Uncle Benjamin said, *"We really can't bother her."*

"Uh. This Daniel Washington lives in Pittsburgh. But maybe it was a large family and Holly has relatives closer to us." She forced herself not to glance toward the kitchen.

But no need, Uncle Benjamin floated into the dining room. He raised his hands above his head. *"She's next to you. Wants to know who your friend is."*

Digger ignored Uncle Benjamin.

Marty frowned. "Maybe, but it's not like this is a big city. Wouldn't she know that?"

Digger shook her head. "We're talking third cousins, at best. Can you name any of yours?"

Marty shook his head slowly. "I don't suppose I can. It would take me a while to figure out if I even know how to find any."

"She's tugging on your elbow."

Digger continued to ignore Uncle Benjamin's words. Without warning, the napkin she had placed next to her elbow when she finished eating slid to the floor. She bent to retrieve it.

"I've never seen her move anything. This is exciting."

When she straightened, Marty regarded her. "Did you push that off the table?"

Digger shut her eyes momentarily. "You said you wanted to believe me, remember?"

"Your...ghost uncle can move napkins?"

"Come on, Cherry. We're interrupting."

"Not him. Cherry."

Marty picked up his half-full wine glass and drained it. When he put it back, his face was unsmiling. "So, your uncle found a ghost child and brought her here."

"Yes. She had almost faded, and…"

There was a tinge of sarcasm to his tone. "But no Samantha?"

"No." Digger drew a breath. "Because she's alive."

He said nothing, so she continued, talking fast. "Last weekend I went back to the cottage. I wanted to see if the raccoon was there, Cherry always asks about him. He was, and he came up to me. I…"

But Marty had stood up. "Digger, I'm your friend. I'll help you. Maybe there are some medicines or something."

She stood, too. "I know it's hard to believe. I barely do. But I can see Uncle Benjamin as clearly as you can see me."

Marty turned and walked toward the front door. "I don't think I'm helping you by listening to your fantasies."

Digger didn't follow him down the hall. If he would just turn back. But the door clicked shut firmly behind him.

CHAPTER
TWENTY-ONE

IT TOOK DIGGER ALMOST a full minute Tuesday morning to remember why she felt so very sad. Marty not only didn't believe her, he thought she was a raving lunatic.

She lay in bed with her eyes shut. She had to stop thinking about him. He wasn't going to be part of her life. A voice in the back of her head told her he could be if she could figure out how to ditch Uncle Benjamin. But that would feel like murder.

She showered quietly, hoping to get out of the house before Cherry got up and started having Uncle Benjamin chatter to Digger on her behalf. She took out a pair of light gray dress slacks and a coral sweater.

Today, she and Holly had a meeting with Abigail and Gene at the Chamber to try to convince him they should start working on a calendar for next year. They would need time to sift through some old-fashioned photographs, take some new ones and, probably the hardest part, convince Gene to pay them to do it.

In the kitchen, Uncle Benjamin sat alone on the Formica-topped table. *"I'm sorry about last night."*

Digger tried to smile but failed. "Maybe he'll end up meeting Samantha someday. That could convince him. At least about the part that she's alive."

"But he'll still think you're nuts."

"Thanks for the ringing endorsement."

"But it's all my fault. If I hadn't come back…"

"I wouldn't have anyone to tell me old stories or hassle me on weekends."

"I mean it," he said.

"I know you do, but it's not just about you." She shrugged. "Maybe it's good to know that he wouldn't believe something important. This probably wouldn't be the only time we'd, I don't know, disagree or think differently."

She wished she could think so logically about it. She couldn't stand the thought of just nodding at Marty if she ran into him around town.

Uncle Benjamin started to say something, but she cut him off. "Holly and I have a three-thirty meeting, I hope it doesn't go too long."

"Why?...Oh, Bitsy. Wish I could open doors."

"Me, too. Keep practicing."

Digger made a sandwich for lunch and headed for her car. Under the windshield wiper rested a piece of paper. Her mood lifted. Maybe Marty had rethought his outburst and wanted to talk more about her so-called fantasies.

She frowned as she read the note. Samantha Halloway wanted to meet at the cottage at two PM.

Digger frowned. She had no way to contact the woman to say that was a very inconvenient time for Digger to be up there. If she wasn't going to believe her daughter was a ghost, why not just go back to New Jersey?

She put her lunch in the car and went back inside to tell Uncle Benjamin about the note. He still sat on the kitchen table.

"You can't mope about this all day."

"Is that what you came back to tell me?"

"No. Samantha wants to meet me at the cottage at two. I feel like I should tell someone I'm going to do that."

"Fat lot of good it'll do you to tell me. I can't pass it on if you don't come home."

"Don't be such a pessimist. Maybe she's changed her mind, she'll meet Cherry, and they'll live happily ever after someplace else."

"I'd like to sort of be a grandpa." He grinned. *"You know, love 'em and give 'em back."*

Digger rolled her eyes. As she walked back through the dining room, she picked up the green folder with the information on Holly's probable great, great grandmother. She shouldn't put off the conversation any longer.

AT LUNCHTIME, HOLLY READ the sheet Digger gave her. "I don't understand."

"If Uncle B...I mean if Marty and I have this right, your second great grandmother was owned by the family that lived next to Hamil Halloway's family. Same house he lives in now. Their name was Hurder, and she used that name. Elizabeth Hurder."

"And she married my great, great grandfather, Charles Washington."

"It seems so. And their great granddaughter-in-law is your grandmother, Audrey Washington." When Holly continued to stare at the paper, Digger added, "May Audrey one day annoy my Uncle Benjamin as much in heaven as she did on earth."

Holly looked up and smiled slowly. "You sure that's where those two will end up?" She leaned back in her chair and closed her eyes.

Digger took a deep breath. "Have you ever seen photos of Charles Washington?"

Her eyes flew open. "Of course not. He died in 1886."

"Yes. Way too young. You said there was no grave, and I never found one either."

"Damn it, a dead end again."

Digger shook her head. "I found some stuff about him on ancestry.com.

"Someone put information on the web?"

"Yep. Looks like a very distant relative. Maybe in another state."

"So why did you ask about a picture?"

Digger opened the green folder and took out a paper. "I printed this from the photo a descendant sent…"

Holly had grabbed the paper and stared at it. "This is him? And her? Elizabeth Hurder?"

Digger nodded. "In 1885. Elizabeth Hurder Washington."

Holly's eyes raised from the paper and met Digger's. "She looks part White. A lot White."

Digger nodded. "I agree. I'm not sure who…"

Holly stood and slammed the paper on the table. "Who her father was? Gee, maybe her mother went to a prayer meeting at the Methodist church in town and met a nice man."

Digger shut her eyes for a moment. "And since that's not likely, it could have been someone in the Hurder family."

"Her owner." Holly's eyes filled with tears and she walked to the window to stare at the street below. Digger heard a car honk, but doubted Holly took in anything.

Digger didn't know what to say. Intellectually, she'd known Holly could have a White ancestor. There were mixed-race families on every census from 1850 forward. To Holly, who styled her hair in what she called the look of a proud Black woman, it might make her question a lot of things.

Softly, Digger said, "I'm sorry it's not what you expected."

In a flat voice, Holly said, "I guess a slave's a slave."

Digger realized she hadn't said more than the woman's name. "Actually, she was on the census as free in 1860. I guess she had been…"

Holly whirled around to face her. "Free? How could she have been free?"

"I can't be sure. Maybe we never will know. Given that she took the Hurder name, my guess was that she'd been manumitted.

ed. Set free." She took a breath. "If she was a daughter of the Hurder family, maybe they wanted her to be free."

With her feet almost stomping, Holly went to her desk and opened the bottom drawer. She took out her purse, didn't grab her coat, and walked to the office door. She opened, walked into the hall, and shut it without a word.

Digger sat very still.

From the other side of the door, Holly said, "Digger? Thank you. I'll see you at three-thirty at the Chamber." Her feet clattered down the steps and the door to the street opened and closed.

Digger sat still for almost a minute. She should have expected this. Of course, Holly liked White people, they were best friends. That didn't mean she wanted to be part White. And maybe it wasn't true.

But it seemed likely. Perhaps Holly would be surprised to find she had more relatives in Maple Grove than just one ornery grandmother.

CHAPTER TWENTY-TWO

DIGGER HIKED RAPIDLY UP the path to the cottage. Why had Samantha's note said to meet on a weekday at two in the afternoon?

Someone, maybe Uncle Benjamin, had said she originally left because her father wouldn't increase her allowance. Maybe she'd found a Sugar Daddy and didn't work.

Her watch said one-fifty, and she and Holly had the meeting at the Chamber at three-thirty. If Samantha showed on time and they didn't talk long, she'd make it.

A pair of squirrels chattered loudly, but she had no human company on the trail.

Digger reached the cottage only mildly out of breath, but saw no sign of Samantha. She faced the cottage back, so walked to the front. She stared at graffiti on the door and shook her head.

Still no one else in sight. "Samantha?" When no one answered, she said, "You don't need to whisper."

She walked to the other side of the cottage and back to the front. She'd never tried to peer in any of the boarded windows, but when she did, she found they were tightly sealed.

Cherry's log was empty, of course, but now wind had swept in a few leaves. Digger straightened and glanced at her watch again. She'd waited ten minutes. She'd give Samantha five more, and then she had to get back. Maybe she'd run into her on the trail.

From the direction of the larger house a car started. Had Samantha gone there? She'd said she hadn't spoken to her father since the day her father tried to strangle her twelve years ago.

Digger moved a few feet to her right so she could better see through the trees. An older sedan, maybe a Buick, pulled away from the house. If Hamil Halloway would be away for a time, she'd walk to that house.

She trudged through a carpet of pine needles and almost tripped over a branch that had been covered in last fall's leaves. At the edge of the mowed area around the large house she stopped. She really had no business being there.

But the house's foundation fascinated her. She couldn't recall seeing dirt packed against a stone and brick foundation the way it was here. It appeared there were windows in some spots because the dirt was sort of indented in two places on the side she faced.

Aloud, she said, "If I were going to hide a body, I'd put it in a cellar. Bury it there, I suppose." If Samantha hadn't moved Cherry, had her grandfather placed her tiny frame down there? Did Cherry's eight-year-old ghost stay in the log to wait for her mother?

Digger walked behind the house and stared at its stark exterior. The shutters in the front gave it a less severe look. A cinderblock patio in the back had buckled slightly. She doubted anyone grilled hot dogs there in the summer.

The set of bulkhead doors that led to the cellar intrigued her. In town, a chain would generally have run between the two handles, but out here Halloway probably figured no one would try to get in. Besides, most exterior cellar entrances led down a short set of stairs that had a traditional doorway at the bottom. That would likely be locked.

From behind her, Hamil Halloway asked, "Looking for something, Ms. Browning?"

She turned, almost tripping as she did. "Oh my God. I didn't realize you were home."

"Obviously." Gone was the genial host she had spoken with a few days ago, replaced by a man flushed with anger. Flushed and holding a shotgun at his side.

"I, I was hiking, and stopped at the cottage."

"And you thought you saw me drive away, so you figured you'd snoop around my house? You didn't think I kept that house clean by myself, did you? You saw a cleaning woman leave."

Digger's breathing had slowed somewhat. "Spur of the moment. I'm sorry. I keep thinking what a perfect spot this would be to hide people. During the Civil War."

"I'm glad you clarified that. I was beginning to think you were looking for the bodies of my daughter and granddaughter."

"I, uh, what? No, of course not. I'm sorry, I should leave."

With the shotgun, he gestured toward the cellar doors. "Why don't you look around the cellar? I promise, there are no cast iron cooking pots, iron bedsteads, or rotting bodies."

"Really, I..."

His voice was flat and adamant. "I insist. Another tour of my home." He gestured again. "The doors aren't locked. Just pull them up."

Digger didn't think she could refuse. She wanted to run. But what was there to be afraid of? Embarrassed, yes. But he wouldn't shoot her. Especially with such a noisy gun. Or would anyone hear him if he did?

DIGGER AWOKE ON A cold, hard floor that had an unexpected smell. What little light available came from a pencil-thin stream from the far side of the place she was in.

She tried to sit up but lay back down. She didn't think her head hurt. She moved it from side to side. Her left shoulder ached, and she thought she remembered falling on it. When she raised a hand to rub it, her left arm hurt at the elbow.

She closed her eyes again and tried to remember what had happened. Slowly it came back. She'd been walking down a short flight of steps. Something hard pushed her in the back. As she fell, she heard a loud noise behind her, and then her forehead hit the floor. She was lucky she hadn't broken her nose.

Digger closed and then opened her eyes again. The world seemed to spin less, so she sat halfway up, putting her weight on her right elbow. After perhaps a minute she sat up fully. Still, she could see nothing except the thin stream of light.

Mystery books always said a person's eyes adjusted to the dark, but that was baloney. Everything to her right, left, and behind her was pitch black. Only the narrow ray of light kept her from thinking she might be blind.

What had she been doing before walking down those steps? She could not bring that to mind, so changed her thinking. Aloud, she said, "Distract yourself. The memory will come back."

Uncle Benjamin floated into her brain and she almost giggled. No one else she knew floated. "Why are you thinking about silly things?" She thought about him finding Cherry and how attentive he'd been to her.

Then she remembered. She'd been at the side of Hamil Halloway's house. Why had she been there? That thought wouldn't come to her, so she concentrated on getting to her feet. She wanted to see where that thin ray of light came from.

She got on her hands and knees and pushed herself up. Her hands felt dirty and she realized she had been lying on a hard-packed dirt floor. Weird. She got gradually to her feet and managed to stay upright.

Digger stumbled toward the thin ray. Amazing how bright it seemed in contrast to the intense darkness of the rest of what seemed to be the Halloway cellar.

When she reached the limestone wall, she could see that a thin window had been buried in dirt. A small space appeared near the bottom of the window. She peered more closely and laughed softly. An acorn. A squirrel had buried a nut and given her a potential lifeline. Or at least the ability to stay sane rather than wallow in the gloom.

With her back leaning against the wall, she surveyed as far as she could into the dark. Then she remembered. Samantha had not shown up at the cottage, so she'd walked to the main house.

Why had Hamil Halloway carried a shotgun? Marty had said something about his irritation at the news article, but why had he pushed Digger into his cellar?

She had no answers. Digger checked her pocket for her phone and pulled it out. She hadn't damaged it in the fall, but no signal. She hadn't expected one, but at least she could have some light if she conserved the battery.

Digger forced herself to think about who knew she'd hiked to the cottage. Only Uncle Benjamin. And he wouldn't know that she had walked from the cottage to the larger house. Though they had talked about it being a more likely stop on the Underground Railroad than the smaller Hurder home. Didn't matter. Uncle Benjamin couldn't tell anyone.

And where did a person go to the bathroom down here? That never seemed to be an issue when a hero was stuffed in a car trunk or closet. More important, she needed water. Although if she didn't get any she wouldn't need to worry about a bathroom. She felt in her fanny pack. She had a ten-ounce bottle of water. Better than nothing.

Footsteps sounded above her, softly, then louder. She couldn't decide if she should call out. No one would know to look for her here, so the sounds had to come from Halloway.

The steps stopped just above her and a little to the left. Maybe the man was listening for her. Digger didn't move. After a short time, the person went back in the direction they'd come from. She didn't realize she hadn't been breathing until she started again.

Digger leaned against the wall and shut her eyes. Even if someone came here to look for her, Halloway had no obligation to let the sheriff or anyone else search the property. And no one would think to look here. By the time anyone did, she could be too weak to yell.

She wished she'd told Holly the file name for the graphic she'd designed for their presentation. She whispered, "That's the least of your worries."

She thought about Uncle Benjamin, frantic at her disappearance and unable to tell anyone where she'd gone. Her eyes started to fill with tears and she wiped them aside. Crying helped nothing.

Marty's face hovered in her brain. Would he be sorry he hadn't believed her?

CHAPTER
TWENTY-THREE

MARTY STARTED AT HIS blank computer screen. He had almost finished an article about the damage graffiti did to natural spaces, specifically, The Knob. He'd suggested it after Sheriff Montgomery told him it would have been good to have a heads up about the earlier piece on the cottage. Montgomery would have had cars pass by the trailhead more often.

He scrolled through photographs he'd taken last week. He wouldn't use one from Saturday, when he'd gone back to The Knob to view the graffiti. It would just encourage the rogue artists. He finally settled on one of the path heading upward, with the boulder in the background.

Then he came across the photo he'd surreptitiously taken of Digger, in profile. He didn't know what to make of her odd behavior. Could Samantha be alive?

Had she been hiding all this time? Was Digger serious, or had she taken a deep dive into the Halloway family and created her own reality?

No one he'd spoken to had raised the possibility of Samantha being alive. They'd known the woman, Digger hadn't. He had begun to think she needed some kind of professional help. Maybe he should ask Franklin if he'd noticed anything unusual about Digger lately.

His office phone rang. "Hofstedder here."

"Hey Marty, it's Holly. Have you seen Digger this afternoon?"

"No. She late or something?"

"She missed a presentation meeting at three-thirty. If she isn't lying somewhere with a broken leg, I'm thinking of giving her one."

Marty said nothing.

"I'm kidding. I'm worried about her. Do you have a key to her place?"

"Uh, no, but she must have one hidden somewhere. You want to ride out with me?" He didn't relish the idea of entering the Ancestral Sanctuary uninvited, not right now, anyway.

"I think I need to stay here. I've made some calls, and people might call me back."

"Sure. I'll head up there."

He sat for a moment after he hung up. Digger had been acting oddly, but she wouldn't lose track of time when she had a meeting. He attached his article to an email and forwarded it to his editor.

He intended to leave without any comment about his destination, but decided to stop at the front counter.

"Hey, Anna. Holly wants me to head up to check on Digger. She missed a meeting, and it's not like her.'

"That's weird."

"Yeah. If she calls, tell her to buzz Holly."

"And you?"

"If she wants. I'll touch base with Holly after I stop at Digger's place."

He could feel Anna's eyes on him as he walked out. She probably wondered why he didn't seem more concerned. It wasn't that. He just figured it was more likely Digger had zoned out than fallen down.

DIGGER HAD LOCATED THE steps that led to the main floor of the house, but she hadn't yet tried to walk up. From the tour Hamil Halloway had given her, she remembered that the basement door led into the kitchen. She didn't recall seeing a bolt, just a handle lock. Minus an ax or crowbar, it would still be hard to get through the door.

Rapid pounding from the front of the house paused her thinking. Halloway didn't seem to be walking in that direction, unless he was now sock-footed. The knocking paused, then continued.

A woman's voice yelled, "I know you're in there! Open up!"

Digger groaned. Samantha. If her father had locked Digger in the cellar, she doubted he'd have any qualms about pulling his shotgun on his daughter.

The pounding continued, and after another minute Digger heard the sound of a chair scraping on the floor in the kitchen. Apparently Halloway had been sitting at the table. He slowly walked to the front of the house.

Perhaps Samantha had seen his image through the door or porch window, because the yelling and battering stopped. Digger held her breath. What would the old man do?

Samantha's "Whoa!" was loud. That was followed by more shouting. Digger thought she heard, "What did you do with my daughter?"

Halloway's response was a harsh laugh, almost a bark. "To the cellar with you."

Digger assumed he had the shotgun pointed at his daughter, because she said, "Backwards. If you're going to shoot me, you'll have to look me in the eye."

From the top of the steps came, "Open it!"

Samantha must have done so because the knob turned. Digger quickly moved out of sight, to the right of the base of the stairs. In a few seconds, Samantha's white sneakers came into view, cautiously climbing backward down the steps.

The momentary shaft of light from the open door vanished with its slam. Silence, not even the sound of Halloway's steps leading away. Then the handle lock snapped.

Samantha kept still on the stairs.

When Halloway moved away, Digger whispered, "Samantha, it's Digger."

Samantha did a sharp intake of breath and responded in a whisper. "Turn on the light."

"I don't know where it is."

Though Digger could no longer see the woman's feet, she heard her turn and come more rapidly down the stairs. "I'll get it." She shuffled around on the floor and Digger sensed movement near her.

A click, and dim light from a single overhead bulb made a circle around Samantha. She studied Digger. "I saw your car. When I couldn't find you, I was afraid he killed you."

"Wish you'd called the sheriff instead of joined me down here."

"Yeah," Samantha's sarcasm dripped. "Because the local sheriff would really come if a dead woman called. After that damn article they'd think it was a prank."

Digger leaned against the wall and rubbed her shoulder. "I take your point."

"Did he hurt you?"

She shook her head. "I think he shoved me down those outside steps and I landed on my shoulder. I wasn't out very long."

Samantha studied her. "He seems so…patrician. But he has a violent streak."

"Is that why you left?"

"After my mother died, he kept saying he should be Cherry's guardian. I finally told him we were going to move away." She closed her eyes briefly. "The day I told him, he was furious, so I came back over here."

"Did Cherry hear him talk about it?"

Samantha walked to the window and examined the dirt before she turned back to Digger. "She was at dance class. Late afternoon the next day, I was loading my car with a couple bags I packed. He must have seen me, because I saw him coming with his stupid shotgun. I ran inside and told Cherry to go out the back door and get into the log where we played hide and seek."

"So, he didn't see her?"

"I told him she had a play date with her friend Tina from her dance class. Then I confronted him about how he bullied me, and I made a big mistake."

"Which was?"

"I told him I thought he pushed Mom down those steps the day she died."

"Did you really think that?"

Samantha shrugged. "She was in great shape, and I didn't think it was all that slippery that morning. He was so angry he dropped his shotgun and reached for my neck to strangle me."

"Good God."

"I got away and ran into the woods. I knew Cherry had heard shouting and would stay put. To be sure, I ran in the opposite direction. I didn't want her to see me and crawl out."

Digger thought about the person Cherry had called the Yeller. "So...you didn't have your car."

"No, but I had the keys so he couldn't move it. A couple times he started to walk back to his place, but he'd come right back."

"So, you couldn't get Cherry?"

She shook her head. "I was worried about her, but she was a tough little cookie. Besides, she'd been tired. I figured she'd fall asleep once it got dark, which was maybe five o'clock." She stopped, her voice choking.

Gently, Digger said, "But it was colder than you expected?"

"Yes. By the time I was sure he was inside for good and went to get her, she had died."

"I'm truly sorry. No one, no parent, should have to go through that."

"I just got in my car and drove for hours. Slept in my car somewhere near the Eastern Shore."

"He could have killed you if you'd gone to him with her body."

She nodded. "Next day he reported us missing. I followed the news. I don't think anyone looked too hard or they would have found her." She looked above her and shouted, "Bastard!"

"Shhh!"

Samantha surveyed the room. "He can hardly hear us up there." She pointed above her head. "Long time ago someone put another layer of wood below the floorboards, so people upstairs weren't likely to hear the slaves down here."

Digger couldn't hide her excitement. "So it *was* a stop on the Underground Railroad."

"That's what my mom said. Her grandmother was from the house that used to be next door." She continued to look around the room, eyes narrowing. "The two families worked together to help slaves get to Pennsylvania."

"Your mom was a Hurder?"

Samantha returned her gaze to Digger. "My great grandmother was. How do you even know that name? That family has been gone from this area for decades, maybe sixty years or more."

"I'll tell you later. Do you know how we can get out of here?"

"Only options are the two doors." She strode toward the exterior door. "Did you look for Cherry's body down here? It's the only place that makes sense."

215

Samantha had reached the door that led to the flight of steps going to the outside bulkhead doors. Digger took out her phone and shone the flashlight as Samantha tried the knob. It turned, but didn't budge.

"He must have propped a two-by-four from the bottom step across to the door. My parents did that when we went out of town. Damn it."

"Samantha, listen to me."

But she turned in a semi-circle. "He had to be the one to take her out of the log, because someone would have found her. I check the *Maple Grove News* online every week."

"From New Jersey?"

"How did…? Oh, my license plate. Yeah, I've been working in a beach town up there for the last ten years."

"And before that?"

"Bummed around. Help me look, would you? He made me give him my phone."

Digger handed her the phone flashlight. "No signal."

"Never was one up here. Still the dark ages." She took the cell phone and shone it around the huge cellar. "There's a couple of almost walled-off areas back here."

Digger followed her to the far side of the cellar. Rough-hewn wood had been propped against the brick and limestone walls. Individual pieces of varied width were fastened together by old metal hinges. Judging by their shape and rust, Digger thought they could be more than one hundred years old.

Samantha handed her the phone. "There's a couple of cubbyholes behind these. My mother said slaves hid here. No one would have dared search this house, but they didn't want anyone looking in the windows."

Digger shone the light at the spot Samantha investigated. "Is that why the soil covers the windows?"

She shook her head as she felt around the piece of wood on the far right. "That's new."

Though the rough panels looked as if they were fastened to the walls, Digger realized there were spike-like nails in only a few of them. The one Samantha grappled with hung at an angle, attached with a hinge to one next to it, which was securely affixed to the bricks.

Samantha pried back the panel and peered behind it. "You can just see one of the holes. They're barely big enough for a person to crawl into. Hand me your phone light again, would you?"

Digger handed it to her and Samantha angled it toward what she had described as a hole. After several seconds, she gasped and the phone fell to the floor. Samantha sank to her knees, saying nothing.

Digger picked up the light and cautiously peered behind the panel. A tiny figure, wrapped like a mummy in a tight blanket and clear plastic, lay next to a Barbie doll.

CHAPTER
TWENTY-FOUR

MARTY WAS NOT LOOKING forward to breaking into Digger's house. He knew there was no spare key. She'd often talked about how many people had one when she inherited the Ancestral Sanctuary.

He pulled into the long driveway. No sign of Digger's Jeep. He almost turned around in the circular front drive, but as he got closer to the house, he could hear Bitsy barking furiously. "Damn it." Wherever Digger was, she didn't mean to leave Bitsy alone after five PM.

The front door was locked, so he made a quick search under a flowerpot and across the rim of the storm door. No key. He started at the sight of Ragdoll when she jumped onto the table by the window.

"Great. Scared of a cat." Accompanied by Bitsy's barking, he walked to the back of the house. After checking for a key, he picked up a garden trowel that sat on the porch and bashed in one of the multiple windowpanes in the door. Bitsy stopped barking.

Marty reached in, turned the bolt, and opened the door. Bitsy escaped and peed for at least ten seconds. Then he bounded back up the steps.

"Whoa. Have to push the glass out of the way." He raised his voice. "Digger?" Surely if she were home, she would have been downstairs by now.

He shoved glass aside with his foot and grabbed a towel from the stove door to push the rest aside. Then he let Bitsy in. The dog walked straight to his empty food bowl. Marty took the bag of dog food from the kitchen pantry and poured some, and added water to that bowl.

Ragdoll walked to the door of the kitchen and stared at him.

"You think this is a restaurant? I don't know where your food is." He opened cabinets until he came to one with cans of cat food and dumped the contents of one onto a saucer. Ragdoll didn't go to it. "Great. Eat at your leisure."

He recognized Digger's family history research files on the dining room table and walked to them. She had a book he hadn't seen about the Underground Railroad, *The Liberty Line*. Next to it were articles about Samantha and Cherry Halloway, including his own.

"She's still thinking about all that."

He walked to Digger's desk in the living room and looked on the wall calendar that sat above it. She had noted the 3:30 meeting, but nothing afterwards.

Next to the desk was her small television set, and he was surprised to see it was on. She must have been watching the news before she left for work and forgotten to turn it off.

He stood in the front hallway and looked back toward the dining room. A single piece of paper sat on the dining room floor. "Odd." He picked up his article on the Halloways and placed it in the middle of the table.

Bitsy barked. "Guess I should check upstairs." The dog followed him into each of the four bedrooms, and the bathroom. He hesitated about going up to Franklin's space in the converted attic, but decided it would be awful if he found out later that she'd gone up there and fallen. No Digger.

He called Holly on his cell phone as he walked back to the first floor. "She isn't here. Are there other friends you can call?"

"I've called everyone I can think of. I'm really worried."

"I'm getting there. I'll drive..." He stopped. He gotten to the dining room. His Halloway article sat on the floor again. He looked around. No one.

"Drive where?" Holly asked.

"She's been really interested in that Halloway cottage. Has she talked to you about it?"

"She actually went up to meet Hamil Halloway at his house last Friday. Didn't she tell you?"

"Huh. It's late. The trails are supposed to be closed, but I guess I'll drive up to that house. You might ask the sheriff to have his guys informally keep an eye out for her."

"I guess I'll do that. Don't stop searching."

"I won't." He hung up and looked around the room. "Okay, Benjamin, if you're here, I'm driving to the Halloway place to see if I can find her."

Bitsy barked. "Stay here, Boy. I'll come back for you if I don't find her. You can stay at my place."

He decided to go to the cottage first, even if the trail did close at dark. In the parking lot at the base of the trailhead sat Digger's car and one with New Jersey plates

"Damn. Where is she?" He moved briskly up the path, nearly half-a-mile to the cottage. The moon had risen some, so he didn't need the flashlight he'd taken out of his glove compartment.

The cottage sat back from the path, and he shone the light around the area. "Digger? Did you fall?" Anyone within a quarter-mile would have to hear him. He moved toward the front of the cottage and halted on hearing the familiar hiss.

He looked down at the raccoon, about fifteen feet from him. "I don't suppose you saw her?"

The raccoon turned and waddled toward a low-hanging pine tree, and then passed it and continued toward the large Halloway home.

Marty tromped around the cottage. On the board covering the front door someone had spray-painted, "You aren't in Kansas anymore."

"Great," he muttered. A stick-figure raccoon had been drawn on the board that covered one front window. Neither could be seen from the path. The so-called artist could actually have been up there in daylight.

He turned, intending to drive to the large house, only to find the raccoon less than six feet from him. "I don't have any food."

It turned and again moved toward the Halloway house. When he didn't immediately follow, it turned and stared at him.

Because the trek to the larger house was overgrown, Marty had planned to drive from the trailhead to the other side of the mountain, which would only take about fifteen minutes. The raccoon seemed to say otherwise. "Okay, I'm following, but you better know the best way through all this brush."

He kept the flash beam about three feet ahead of him and occasionally stooped to walk under a low-hanging branch. If he hadn't had the light, he probably would have scratched his glasses on a couple of them.

As he grew closer, what had been a pen-prick of light became a ginger lamp in the living room window. No front porch light, but he hadn't expected a welcome mat. He climbed onto the porch and knocked on the door. No answer.

He found the doorbell and tried it, but still Hamil Halloway didn't appear. In other circumstances, he'd have left, because if the man had a car, it was in a detached garage on the side of the property and he couldn't see if Halloway was home or out.

He knocked again, and eventually saw a curtain move to the right of the door. It opened.

Hamil Halloway turned on the porch light, opened the door, and stood, unsmiling, as he regarded Marty.

"I'm sorry to bother you, sir."

Halloway peered beyond him. "Car trouble?"

"What? No. My car's in the lot, near the trailhead. I'm Martin Hofstedder, and…"

Halloway made to shut the door.

"Wait, please. I'm not here as a reporter. I'm looking for my friend, Digger Browning."

"Miss Browning? I met her last week. She's certainly not here now."

Marty pushed his glasses back up his nose. "I didn't really think she would be, but we're trying anything. She seems to be missing. She didn't call, or come by earlier, did she?"

Halloway frowned, but seemingly more in concern than anger. "No. She's a nice young woman. If I see her, how do I contact you?"

Marty fished in his pocket for a business card. "My cell number is on the back of this *Maple Grove News* card. I'd appreciate a call if you see her. Or tell her to call me or Holly, her business partner."

Halloway extended his hand and regarded the card.

"I promise, no reporting."

Halloway smiled. "I hope you find your friend." He shut the door firmly but did leave on the porch light.

Marty walked slowly down the steps and spotted the raccoon about twenty feet away. "Crazy animal," he muttered. He had gone less than ten yards when he thought he heard muffled voices. "What the hell?"

He turned slightly, saw Halloway at the window, waved, and made for the woods to go back to the cottage. The porch light went out, and he stopped a few feet past the mowed lawn and regarded the house.

IN THE CELLAR, Digger has been kneeling next to Samantha, trying to comfort her. "I have some water in my fanny pack, take a sip."

Samantha, head still between her knees, shook her head.

Digger settled next to her on the floor. "I'm sorry you had to find her."

Samantha turned so she stared at Digger's elbow. "I knew he had to be the one who moved her. I just hope to hell it's been half as hard on him." She sniffed loudly. "I never should have left her in that log."

"It was a play space for her, and she was safe."

Samantha stared at her dirty sneakers. "It never occurred to me that it was that cold."

Digger couldn't blame a mother for wanting to hide her daughter from a man with a shotgun, even if it was a relative. Everyone she'd spoken to said Samantha the wild teenager changed when Cherry was born. She'd been a good mother.

"Can I ask you a question?"

Samantha shrugged. "Not much else to do."

"Who was the man Cherry calls the Yeller?"

Samantha shivered. "So, you really do see her ghost?"

"Uncle Benjamin does. He tells me what she says."

"He talked loud a lot, but we didn't actually fight. This guy named Karl Hindberg. He kept trying to talk me into leaving here. Cherry hated to hear people argue."

Digger debated saying she'd met him, but went ahead. "I talked to him a few days ago. He sounded like a good friend."

"If only I'd listened to him." Samantha's voice broke.

"Sure you don't want some water?"

Samantha sat up and leaned against the wall. "Yeah, thanks. Have any food?"

Digger opened her fanny pack. "We can split a granola bar." She uncapped the water.

Samantha tilted her head back and took a drink without touching the rim of the plastic bottle. She handed it back. "That'll hold me."

Digger split the granola bar and handed her half. "I had lunch. We might want the other half later."

Samantha chewed slowly, saying nothing.

"Why did you come here?" Digger asked. "Were you actually looking for me?"

She nodded. "I saw your car. Sorry I was late."

"If I'd walked to my Jeep instead of snooping at this house, we wouldn't be down here."

"Will anyone look for you later?"

"I missed a three-thirty meeting, but my partner won't think to have anyone check up here." Uncle Benjamin certainly couldn't send a search party.

A knocking sound made both of them sit up straight. Digger turned to Samantha. "Would he call someone to help, I dunno, get rid of us?"

"I have no idea what he would do."

The doorbell rang and they both stood. Someone knocked again and it sounded as if the front door opened. Without saying anything, they walked to the bottom of the steps.

Digger whispered. "I think I can hear talking, but no words."

After less than a minute, the door closed.

"Let's yell," Samantha said. They ran the short distance to what Digger now thought of as the squirrel window."

"Here! We're down here!"

No response.

"Come back!"

Halloway pounded on the door from upstairs. "Be quiet! No one is here."

Samantha muttered, "Then why do you care?" But she didn't yell again. "It would be easy for him to shoot us. A shotgun blast splatters lots of directions."

Digger turned her ear toward the window. "I think someone's out there." She tapped on the glass with her knuckles.

Then came a scratching sound, and Digger realized someone was trying to pry dirt away from the window. Samantha turned to her and they hugged.

In a normal tone of voice, Digger said, "We're down here."

The fumbling at the dirt continued. "Digger? Is that you?"

"Yes! Marty?"

"Yeah." He had cleared a spot about two inches square and peered in. "Can't you get out?"

"We're locked in," Samantha said.

"Who are you with?"

Samantha looked at Digger. "He'll never believe it."

Digger said, "Samantha. Long story. Can you get the sheriff or something?"

"There's no phone signal. I don't think I should leave you."

"Walk around back," Samantha said.

After a pause, he said, "Okay. Another door?"

"Yes," Digger said, "But he has a shotgun."

"Crud."

His feet made little sound on the grass as he moved away. Digger and Samantha stood still for several seconds, listening. They exchanged a look, Samantha shrugged, and they walked across the room to the exit that led to the bulkhead doors above.

"They aren't locked outside," Digger said to Samantha.

"I know, but they might creak."

After another minute, the door above opened and Marty quickly shut it. He turned on a flashlight as he came down the steps.

"We see you," Digger said, softly.

"There's cinderblocks stretched from the bottom step to your door." He began moving them. "Are you locked in from your side?"

"No," Samantha said. "When the blocks are gone, we can get out."

"Try it," Marty said.

The door swung out and Marty stepped in. Digger went to him and he grabbed her in a hug.

"Hugs later," Samantha said. "We have to hurry."

Marty let go of Digger and regarded Samantha. "Welcome home."

She smiled, briefly. "Not yet. Come on." She led the way to the short flight of steps and gingerly pushed on the bulkhead door. As she did, a single shot rang out.

"Crap." She shut it.

"Didn't sound like a shotgun," Digger said.

"A twenty-two. Get back in here," Marty said. He beckoned them into the cellar.

"Not safe," Digger said.

"He can't be two places at once," Marty said.

Samantha shook her head. "Yeah, but the door he's firing from is near the door to the cellar. He's got us boxed in."

They stood inside, near the door.

"Do you think one of us could get out?" Digger asked. "Get through to the trail, I mean?"

"Risky," Marty said.

"But whatever we do, we should do it fast, before he has time to think about what to do with us," Samantha said.

"I'll call up to him from the bottom of the steps," Digger said. "When we can tell he's just on the other side of the upstairs door, Samantha can run to the trail and get down to her car."

"Why her? I should do it," Marty said.

"I'm the smallest target, and I know the area best."

Digger took her phone from her pocket. "Take this so you can call the sheriff."

"Thanks." She gestured to the steps going upstairs. "Get busy." She walked through the door, and they watched her crouch on the cement steps going up to the bulkhead doors.

Digger and Marty walked across the cellar. "Mr. Halloway," she called.

Nothing.

Marty tried. "Hamil, what do you think you can accomplish? People know where to look for us."

"At least talk to us," Digger said.

"Where's my daughter?"

They heard Samantha start to open the bulkhead doors. Marty raised his voice. "She doesn't want to talk to you."

Digger yelled, too. "She found Cherry."

Marty faced her, eyes wide. "Cherry?"

The bulkhead door closed with a thud and they heard Halloway move quickly to the back door.

"Don't let him shoot her," Digger whispered.

From above came the resounding blast of a shotgun.

CHAPTER
TWENTY-FIVE

DIGGER GRABBED MARTY'S ARM. "He's probably a lousy shot."

Halloway clattered down the outside stairs that ran from the back porch to the yard.

Digger and Marty dashed across the room. Marty reached out the door and threw two cinder blocks into the room and Digger slammed the door as he hurled himself in after them.

But Halloway wasn't coming for them – yet. Digger turned the door lock. They heard him pass the bulkhead doors.

Marty pointed upstairs. "Run!"

She tore up the steps ahead of him. At the same time, they realized they were still locked in.

Marty leaned against the wall and kicked. The door didn't unlock, but the thin wood began to splinter. He kicked again. More splintering. He grabbed his knee.

"Move!" She leaned against the wall at the other side of the stairs, raised a leg and kicked just below the doorknob. She felt the interior latch on the plate start to give and kicked again. With a bang the door opened.

"I loosened it," Marty said.

Digger grunted a laugh and made for the living room. Marty paused and turned the handle lock on the door to the back porch.

"Good thinking," Digger panted. She turned off the lone lamp in the living room. "Out the front door?"

"If I get down the steps, follow me." He crouched, unlocked the front door, and went out the door without pause.

Halloway rattled the handle of the back door. He yelled, but Digger could only tell it had to be a curse.

Marty bolted down the front steps as Halloway clambered down the back ones. Digger realized if Marty turned right, he could run into the older man.

"Go left," she screamed.

But he must have gone right because another blast reverberated through the night.

Marty changed directions and ran across the front of the house at a sprint.

"Let him be faster. Let him be faster." She stayed inside. By the time she started to run for the trees in the direction of the cottage, Halloway would be too close.

He came to the side of the house nearest the front door and Digger slammed it and locked the bolt.

Another shotgun blast rang out, but Halloway swore again.

"He missed, he missed. Let him miss."

She turned fully. She was locked in the Halloway house, but the old man could blast his way in. A set of stairs, bare wood with oriental-style carpet strips on each one, led upstairs. Digger tore up them.

At the top she stopped, panting. The only light came from the end of the hall, a dim one that could have been a reading lamp. She didn't want to turn on any more. She made her way down the hall and entered what looked to be the master bedroom. The curtains weren't closed so she edged to the lamp on a bedside table and flicked it off.

She crawled into the hallway and glanced in both directions. Grand old houses always had a back staircase, but she hadn't seen one leading into the kitchen. The butler pantry had had two doors. If one led to the dining room, maybe the other led to a narrow staircase to the second floor. But how to access it from up here?

In the stillness, Digger heard the bolt click on the front door. Halloway must have had his keys with him. She didn't have to hide forever, just long enough for Marty or Samantha to get a cell signal and call the sheriff.

Even if Montgomery or his deputies thought Samantha's call was a crank call, they'd believe Marty. If he hadn't been shot.

"Miss Downing. I know you're in here."

Digger stood. She had to find those back stairs.

MARTY HEARD PELLETS FROM the shotgun whiz near him and ran full tilt. He almost fell twice before he made it half the distance to the cottage. The second time he lay on the ground, heart pounding. No one seemed to be running behind him.

He crouched and stumbled the rest of the way to the cottage and ran behind it. He peered out, eyes adjusting to the moonlight that filtered between the leaves. After a minute, he decided Halloway would have wanted to try to keep Digger in his house.

Marty began to run down the path, but halted abruptly at what looked to be a large rock in front of him. "Damn!" He stooped next to Samantha. Blood ran down the side of her face.

"I'm mostly okay. I think it just grazed my head."

"Let me help you up."

"No." She sat up and leaned on an elbow. "Walk me off the path. You'll go faster alone."

He helped her stand. She leaned on him, but could walk. "You still have Digger's phone, right?"

"Yes, but the signal's too weak to call."

"As long as the light works. If I don't see you when I come back, you can flash it." He shone his own on her head after she sat against a tree a few feet away from the trail. "You're right. Not deep."

"I think the blood scared me and I went too fast..." her voice trailed off.

Marty squeezed her elbow. "I'll be back."

He looked both ways down the path and began running. In another quarter-mile he reached the parking lot and pulled his phone from his pocket. "Be a signal. Be a signal." Only two bars. "Damn."

He dialed 9-1-1. "What's [static] your [static}?"

"This is Marty Hofstedder. Send deputies to the Halloway place on the west side of the Mountain. Man with a gun."

"Send them [static]?"

"Damn it to hell." He beeped his car open and tore out of the lot. When half-a mile closer to town he stopped and checked the phone. Three bars. He tried again.

"9-1-1. What's the nature of your emergency?"

"The Halloway place on the west side of the mountain. There's a man...I don't know the address. Hamil Halloway. Look it up! I'm trying to tell you Hamil Halloway has a shotgun and possibly a hostage in his home."

He began driving again. He'd go across the top of the town and up the west side of the mountain. It would be faster than hiking back to the cottage and running across to the house.

"Who is this?"

"Marty Hofstedder. *Maple Grove News.* You're looking for Digger Downing, right? She's at the Halloway place. He has a gun."

"You have Ms. Downing?"

Marty felt as if his head would explode. "I'm trying to tell you she's hiding in the Halloway house. Sheriff Montgomery, the other deputies know where it is, above Maple Grove. You have to hurry."

The dispatcher started to ask for the address again. Marty hung up. On TV, if a call got interrupted, they sent police right away. Maybe that would be faster.

DIGGER COULD HEAR Halloway walking through the first floor. It helped her picture it and get a sense of what part of the second floor would be above the butler pantry.

In the middle of the upstairs hallway, one door was shut. A closet, perhaps? The attic trap door sat above it, but she'd be stuck up there with no options. With the lights out, she felt safe standing and moved to the closet. "Please don't let it squeak," she whispered.

She opened it and faced a huge dumbwaiter. She figured it had been a narrow staircase from the pantry to the second floor. It had to be electric. She peered in and saw a switch and noted the dumbwaiter had a ceiling.

Halloway had been in the kitchen and was coming toward the front of the house, near the main staircase. She climbed into the dumbwaiter and gently pulled the door shut. If she timed it right, if she heard him close to the dumbwaiter door she could start down, maybe stop midway.

Then she realized he probably had a switch down below. But he couldn't be in two places at once. And a shotgun blast might go through the ceiling of the dumbwaiter, but he had to know Marty or Samantha would bring help. Did he want a body rattling around in his walls?

The image of little Cherry's body wrapped in a blanket made her realize he didn't care. He must be mad. If he found his little granddaughter's body in a log, why not call the sheriff or EMTs? Did he think Samantha would come back to look for her daughter if no one found her?

Digger remembered that Samantha said she'd accused him of pushing her mother down the steps. Did he think if he said nothing about Cherry that Samantha would return, and he could have it out with her? Perhaps accuse her of abandoning her daughter and causing her death? Maybe then he'd get the life insurance money Anita Halloway left for Cherry's education.

Halloway's voice carried from downstairs. "I know you're up there, Miss Downing. Digger." He said her first name like a sneer. "You didn't get away. I watched from the edge of the lawn."

Digger's heart beat so loudly it seemed to vibrate in her ears. She shut her eyes and kept her hand on the doorknob.

Halloway came partway up the stairs. Digger figured he could see at least somewhat down the hallway.

"Turned out all the lights. That was smart."

How long had Marty been gone, and how fast could he run? Did he get a signal in the trailhead parking lot?

Halloway had reached the top of the staircase. "You can't hide for long." His voice grew more distant.

Digger figured he had walked into one of the bedrooms. She thought there were two between the top of the steps and the dumbwaiter. He opened and closed a door. Probably the bedroom closet.

Back in the hallway, he said, "I'm coming for you."

Crazy. The man had surely lost his mind. He walked into the second bedroom and opened and closed two doors.

Digger opened her eyes. The total darkness had seemed reassuring when she climbed into the dumbwaiter. Not so now. She felt for the switch. She should have kept her hand on that instead of the doorknob.

Panic. No, she found it. Thank God it was in the compartment with her and not on the door jamb or wall. She had been holding her breath and let it out.

As Halloway came back into the hallway, Digger pressed the switch to take the dumbwaiter down.

"Ah ha!" He came closer and opened the closet door, but by that time the dumbwaiter had moved down enough that he could only see the top of it.

Digger stopped it and spread herself, spider-like, against its walls. She'd be less of a target.

Above her, Halloway's laugh rang jubilant. "You think you're smart." He racked his shotgun.

Digger held her breath. Then she heard tires screeching somewhere near the house.

Halloway swore and moved toward the stairway. From her spot within the house's walls, she could hear his footsteps. For an older man, he moved fast. The front door opened. Surely he had gone out.

Digger pushed the switch again and the dumbwaiter made its way to the first floor. As she climbed into the pantry she could hear shouting outside at the front of the house, but couldn't discern the words. "Please don't shoot," she whispered.

BLAM!

"Oh, no." She started to leave the pantry and run onto the back porch, but the front door opened again.

Halloway breathed so hard she could hear him. She looked around. No butcher block holder of knives, not that she would stand a chance with a blade. She grabbed two cans of soup from the pantry shelf and turned the knob on the door that led to the dining room.

As Halloway entered the pantry and fired his shotgun, she dove through the door into the dining room. She landed on her hands and knees and slammed the door shut with her foot. Amid the noise of the gun and the acrid smell of powder, she heard sirens.

At the same time the front door opened. Marty yelled, "Digger."

From the kitchen, the shotgun blasted again.

Marty yelled. Was he shot?

She ran into the dining room proper. As Halloway came from the kitchen, she lobbed a can of soup, striking him on the side of the head. He turned toward her, only mildly stunned, and she threw the other can as hard as she could.

Knocked off balance, Halloway stumbled. He held onto the gun, but with only his right hand, which dropped to his side.

Digger raced across the room. She dove for the gun and forced it to the floor. As she did, Marty ran from the front of the house and landed partially on her and the gun and partially on Halloway.

"Stay down!" Marty yelled.

From the front yard, a man called, "Come out without the gun!"

Halloway struggled and Marty leaned back and slugged him in the face. His head hit the floor and he covered his bleeding nose with one hand.

Digger kept her hand on the shotgun as Marty stood and pulled her to her feet. As heavy footsteps came up the front porch, she sat the gun on the floor a few feet from Halloway.

Marty looked down at the man below them and then at her. "Honest to God, no one ever shot at me until I met you."

CHAPTER TWENTY-SIX

DIGGER SAT ON THE front steps as EMTs attended to Halloway. She had wanted to go with Marty to get Samantha, but Sheriff Montgomery sent Deputy Charlie Collins with him and told her to stay put.

She rested her head on her knees, shut her eyes, and tried to figure out what had drawn Marty to the Halloway house. Even if Holly had mentioned that Digger had visited here last week, it seemed odd that he would come here.

The front door opened and Montgomery stepped onto the porch. "They're going to transport him to the hospital in Oakland. He says you attacked him."

Digger looked up. "Only if you can call throwing soup cans at him after he shot at me an attack."

Montgomery motioned that she should stand. "Walk onto the lawn with me while they bring him out."

In the house behind them, Digger could hear the two EMTs talking and the squeak of the gurney's wheels as they trundled across the beautiful hardwood floors. She followed Montgomery down the steps and about twenty yards away from the porch.

Halloway lay on the gurney, his neck in a huge brace, patches of blood on the collar of his crisp white shirt.

Montgomery turned his head. "Samantha Halloway is really alive?"

"He locked the two of us in the cellar. Before Marty got here."

"How'd you hook up with her?"

"I guess she drove down here…"

"From where?"

"Jersey shore."

He grunted.

"Anyway, she read Marty's article, and for some reason came back to the cottage." Digger paused. How could she possibly explain this without sounding insane? "She saw me and – I never asked her this – maybe followed me to the Ancestral Sanctuary."

"She been staying with you a couple days?"

"God no. I mean, I have no idea where she went. Today she left a note on my car and told me to meet her up here." She sighed. "Did you go down to the cellar?"

He nodded, grimly, as the ambulance pulled away. "Do you know how long ago the child died?"

"According to Samantha, she told her to hide in a log by the cottage. She heard her father coming and knew he was furious, and had that shotgun. Samantha got away, but she didn't realize how the cold would affect Cherry. When she came back for her, Cherry had died. Hypothermia, I guess."

"This is going to be a heck of a thing to straighten out."

"I believe her."

He started toward the house again. "For some reason, my grandmother thinks you have some insight into all of this."

"She does?"

"Holly called to see if you were over there and she called me. Since you're usually free to bug me, and you hadn't, I was thinking of asking a doctor to check on Grandmother Maryann. She sounded off her rocker."

Digger sighed. "Not as much as you're going to think I am."

MARTY HAD DRIVEN SAMANTHA back to the Halloway house in her car. She refused to go to the hospital. The EMTs finally agreed that she didn't seem to have a concussion. Scalp wounds simply bled a lot.

Sheriff Montgomery and Digger stood outside the car, and he regarded Samantha. "I'm very sorry about your daughter, Samantha. It's almost nine o'clock, and you look like hell. I can wait until tomorrow to talk to you if you can show me some ID and stay...well, not here, in the area tonight."

Samantha looked at Digger.

"Sure, plenty of room. Will probably smell bad, my dog didn't get out this evening."

"I let him out," Marty said.

"How did you get in?"

"I broke a windowpane in your back door."

"Believe that's happened before," Montgomery said.

Digger thought he smirked. To Marty, she said, "Thanks. I think."

"Thank Holly."

Digger hadn't given her a thought. "She must be worried sick."

"I had Dispatch call and tell her you're more or less okay," Montgomery said. "She said she has a fierce headache and not to call her tonight."

Digger felt guilty. She should have at least told Holly where she was going.

"Hofstedder, come to the station and make a statement. Digger can get Samantha settled and," Montgomery nodded to Digger, "you two come by early tomorrow to talk to me."

"Yes, sir."

"We can't do much more tonight." Montgomery walked back into the Halloway house.

Digger, Marty, and Samantha looked at each other. Digger finally spoke to Marty. "How did you think to come here?"

"When I went to your house, a copy of my update article about the cottage fell on the floor. Twice." He looked at Samantha.

She said, "Digger told me some stuff. Is it true?"

He made an exaggerated shrug. "I don't know which end is up."

"You still don't believe me?" Digger asked.

"I believe something, but I don't know what." He stepped to Digger and they hugged. He whispered. "It'll definitely have to be my place."

Digger leaned against his shoulder and smiled.

DESPITE SAMANTHA SAYING she felt fine, Digger didn't think she should drive after she'd been unable to run down the path to the trailhead. Digger used Samantha's car to drop Marty at his car in the trailhead lot and drove to the Ancestral Sanctuary with Samantha. With all the sheriff activity, her Jeep would be safe in the lot overnight.

When they got to the top of the town, Digger kept driving toward a gas station.

"Where are we going?" Samantha asked.

"To get a couple bottles of water so you can wash the blood out of your hair, in case your daughter can see you."

"Oh, right. I have a clean shirt in the trunk. I probably look like a freak."

Digger smiled. "No, but kind of scary with the blood. Stay in the car. We can pull off the road near my place and you can change your shirt and rinse out your hair."

"Good thinking."

They pulled into the overlook near the Ancestral Sanctuary about ten, and Samantha cleaned herself up and combed her hair so the bandage on the side of her forehead didn't show too much.

"How do I look?"

"Like a tired mom. I hope you can both see each other."

"Maybe she'll be asleep."

"That would be good. We can find out if you can see her before she wakes up."

"This is complicated."

"Yep. You'll see her and I'll see Uncle Benjamin."

"Oh, right. Your uncle." Samantha leaned against the passenger seat. "I'm really nervous."

"It'll be easier than getting shot at."

The Ancestral Sanctuary was dark when they pulled up. Digger decided she would always leave a light on in the house from now on. Bitsy began to bark as soon as she parked.

Samantha smiled. "The dog Marty let out."

"Yep. Bitsy." Digger ran up the porch step, unlocked the door, and flipped on the porch and hallway lights at the same time. Bitsy ran out.

Uncle Benjamin, almost transparent, floated to her. *"I wish to heck I could hug you."*

"Are you okay? You're so pale."

"Had to push the damn letter on the floor twice before that boyfriend of yours got the right idea. He...is this Samantha?"

Digger turned. "Uncle Benjamin is tired, but happy to see you. Can you see him?"

She shook her head. "Where is Cherry?"

"Upstairs in bed." Uncle Benjamin started up the steps.

Digger shut the front door and turned the lock. "We're following Uncle Benjamin upstairs. Cherry's room is the second one down the hall, and the cat sleeps with her a lot. I hope you can see more than Ragdoll on the bed."

"Rag...oh, the cat." She climbed slowly, behind Digger.

At the bedroom door, Samantha's face lit up and she suddenly looked like the carefree young woman on the missing persons flyer from twelve years ago. She whispered, "I can see her."

Digger didn't follow her into the room. "I'll be next door. My cousin's old bedroom is on the other side of the bathroom. Use that if you want."

Samantha entered Cherry's room and shut the door behind her.

Digger pointed downstairs. "I'm hungry. Are you okay to go down the steps again?"

"I've regained most of my strength." He floated beside her into the kitchen. *"I wish I could learn how to move solid objects without fading so much."*

"I suppose you could have an eternity to practice."

MARTY SHOWED UP AT eleven, as Digger was about to go upstairs to bed. She let him in and they stood in the front hallway and kissed until Digger felt breathless.

She pulled away. "I can't believe we made it through all that."

He grinned. "Where is your uncle?"

Uncle Benjamin's voice drifted down from above. "I'm going to Franklin's apartment and staying there until you say I can come down. Or Cherry comes up to get me in the morning."

Digger smiled and repeated what he said.

"Samantha upstairs?"

"Yes, and she can see Cherry, who's sleeping."

He shook his head. "That's almost more than I can handle."

Digger could hear the humor in his voice. "I'd like to be more than you can handle. Come into my living room lair."

CHAPTER TWENTY-SEVEN

DIGGER SAT IN THE Coffee Engine Wednesday afternoon to read Marty's *Maple Grove News* website article. His editor had looked into printing a one-page special edition for what he had captioned: "The biggest Maple Grove story of the century." But since it would only be one day earlier than the regular Friday edition, he gave up on the idea.

Uncle Benjamin read over Digger's shoulder. *"I hope Marty reminded him that it's relatively early in the century."*

Since she wasn't about to respond in a public place, Digger murmured, "Mmm."

LOCAL MAN ARRESTED FOR ATTEMPTED MURDER

Sheriff Roger Montgomery arrested Hamil Halloway Tuesday evening for firing, with intent to kill, at two current and one former resident of Maple Grove. Also discovered in his cellar was the body of his long-missing granddaughter, Cherry Halloway. Tentatively the county medical examiner believes she died of natural causes twelve years ago, but an autopsy is pending.

The article described the "reemergence" of Samantha Halloway and how she had told her daughter to hide in the log to be safe from Hamil Halloway, whom she said had also tried to kill her twelve years ago.

Digger had just finished reading Sheriff Montgomery's statement that "no charges were pending for Ms. Halloway" when Holly came in and plopped in a chair across from Digger.

Digger began to stand. "Was I supposed to be back already?"

Holly pointed to Digger's chair. "Sit, woman. I put the answering system on. I was tempted to say something like we were away on spring break, but I said that we'd be back tomorrow."

Digger smiled. "It isn't as if the calls are about design work."

"Definitely not." Holly raised a finger to Amber behind the counter. "How about a café au lait, with sugar?"

"Coming up."

"Any significance in your choice?" Digger asked.

"Hush. I'm still getting over my worry headache."

"I really am sorry I scared you."

"I know." Holly sighed. "I stopped by Audrey's before I came over here. She said she'd looked into Grandfather Daniel's side some. She thought Charles Washington's wife was Elizabeth, but she claims not to have known Elizabeth was a Hurder."

"Does it matter if she did know?

Uncle Benjamin positioned himself cross-legged on a table next to Digger and Holly. *"I bet she knew."*

"I'm not sure," Holly nodded a thank you to the barista as she placed the coffee in front of her. "I guess it mostly matters if she knew and made me keep looking. You know, hoping I'd never figure out I had White ancestors."

Digger grinned. "Some of us are okay."

Holly rolled her eyes. "I'm sorry I got angry yesterday. I think it was more because I thought somebody in my family should have told me, not you.'

"It was so long ago, and a couple of those Washington men died at about fifty or younger. Besides," she shrugged, "Probably it was just accepted." She paused. "In that photo of Charles and Elizabeth Washington, they look happy."

Uncle Benjamin winked at her. *"That's what counts."*

"True. Now I have to decide if I want to see how many other cousins I have."

"That folder I gave you has the contact info for the guy who was a DNA match to you."

Holly grinned. "I already sent him an email."

The Coffee Engine door opened again and Marty came in. "The dream team."

Digger patted a chair next to her.

"I'm going to take my coffee to go," Holly said.

"Don't you dare," Marty said. "I'll get some iced tea and join you."

"Get me one, too," Uncle Benjamin called to him. He winked at Digger.

Holly took a big swallow of her drink and nodded to Digger. "Actually, Audrey's meeting me at the historical society. I want her to look at that book of stories you found. I think it would be really cool if some of our family helped people escape on the Underground Railroad."

"Uncle Benjamin wanted me to do a history on that. For this area, I mean. Maybe you should do it."

She stood, taking her cup. "If you're good I'll let you help." She waved at Marty and left.

"She could do a good one."

Digger glanced in Uncle Benjamin's direction and raised her eyebrows.

"I'm going to wait outside." He floated through the door.

Marty sat, eyes on Holly as she walked past the large window. "I didn't scare her away, did I?"

"Nope. She's meeting Audrey to look at some of the history stuff at the society."

"Good." He leaned closer. "Are we alone?" He put his hand over hers on the table.

Digger smiled. "He wanted to come into town, but he's outside."

"Giving us some privacy?"

"Yep. And letting Samantha and her little friend have the house to themselves."

Marty put his chin on his chest and raised it again. "This is a lot to take in, you know."

"It is. After things get sorted out, it'll just be Uncle Benjamin. This morning," Digger glanced around to see if anyone could hear her, "Samantha said she's thinking of moving into the cottage, and Cherry apparently told her to move the cottage to be closer to Uncle Benjamin."

"Hmm. Be tough to move it, but there aren't zoning laws where you are. Maybe you could build a small place on your property."

Digger shrugged. "I'm doing one day at a time for most of it. Samantha also likes where she's been living in New Jersey, and she's been talking to Cherry about living some here and some at the beach. Apparently, they both loved making sandcastles."

Marty took a sip of coffee. "I didn't pester Samantha when I drove her back to the Halloway place last night. But she did say she sent me this weird email I got last week. It just said to 'leave it alone.'"

"What?"

"Her and the cottage. It was right after the article. God, was that only last Friday?"

Digger smiled. "Time flies."

"Hey, do ghosts fly?"

A woman who was making her way to the counter stared at Marty, and Digger giggled. "We're planning a haunted house."

Marty nodded to Digger. "She's going to live in it."

The woman gave a distracted smile and continued on to order her drink.

Digger grinned and spoke in a low tone. "See how hard it is to deal with normal conversation?"

"I'm getting the point."

"They float."

He rubbed the side of his face. "Does Franklin know?"

Digger sighed. "My next big task. I mean, if you know, I have to tell him."

"Will he believe you?"

Digger glanced toward the window, where Uncle Benjamin stood facing the street. "I sure hope so. His dad can probably think of a way to convince him."

"What do you mean?"

"Tell me something to tell Franklin, something I wouldn't know otherwise."

"Ah. Good idea. I have another one."

"What's that?"

He grinned. "My place tonight."

"I'm all for it."

THE END

Other Books by Elaine L. Orr

The Jolie Gentil Cozy Mystery Series.
Appraisal for Murder
Rekindling Motives
When the Carny Comes to Town
Any Port in a Storm
Trouble on the Doorstep
Behind the Walls
Vague Images
Ground to a Halt
Holidays in Ocean Alley
The Unexpected Resolution
The Twain Does Meet (novella)
Underground in Ocean Alley
Aunt Madge and the Civil Election (long short story)
Jolie and Scoobie High School Misadventures (prequel)

River's Edge Mystery Series
From Newsprint to Footprints
Demise of a Devious Neighbor
Demise of a Devious Suspect

Logland Mystery Series
Tip a Hat to Murder
Final Cycle
Final Operation

Family History Mystery Series
Least Trodden Ground
The Unscheduled Murder Trip
Mountain Rails of Old

Bio for Elaine L. Orr

Elaine L. Orr authors four mystery series, including the eleven-book Jolie Gentil cozy mystery series, set at the Jersey shore. *Behind the Walls* was a finalist for the 2014 Chanticleer Mystery and Mayhem Awards. The three-book River's Edge cozy mystery series is set in Iowa, and *Demise of a Devious Neighbor* was a 2017 Chanticleer finalist. The three-book Logland series takes place in small-town Illinois. Elaine also writes plays and novellas, including the one-act, *Common Ground*, and novellas *Falling Into Place* and *In the Shadow of Light*. A novella, *Biding Time*, was one of five finalists in the National Press Club's first fiction contest, in 1993. Nonfiction includes *Monett* and *Writing When Time is Scarce*.

Elaine conducts presentations on publishing and other writing-related topics. She also blogs on writing and publishing and presents her musings at *Irish Roots Author* (found at htttp://elaineorr.blogspot.com). A member of Sisters in Crime, Elaine grew up in Maryland and moved to the Midwest in 1994.

http://www.elaineorr.com
For Elaine's monthly newsletter go to
http://eepurl.com/crf3F1

For articles on reading, writing, and publishing, check out http://elaineorr.blogspot.com

Made in the USA
Monee, IL
27 September 2022

14683690R00144